D1395792

Sabine

Sabine

A.P.

BLOOMSBURY

Copyright © 2005 by A. P.

The moral right of the author has been asserted

Bloomsbury Publishing Plc, 38 Soho Square, London W1D 3HB

A CIP catalogue record for this book
is available from the British Library

ISBN 0 7475 7856 7

10 9 8 7 6 5 4 3 2 1

Typeset by Hewer Text Ltd, Edinburgh
Printed in Great Britain by Clays Ltd, St Ives plc

All papers used by Bloomsbury Publishing are natural,
recyclable products made from wood grown in well-managed
forests. The manufacturing processes conform to the
environmental regulations of the country of origin

For Ali and Sarah

Once the mark is branded
on the victim's skin,
the little green door opens
and, soundless, beckons in.

On the grassy threshold
gleams my blood like sap.
Night, oh, come and crown me
with a dunce's cap.

– from '*Heimweg*'
by Ingeborg Bachmann

1

Overture

France. The château country inside it. The château itself inside the country, and Aimée and us inside the château. Five non-students, in a non-school, run by a non-teacher with no qualifications at all, bar one, and that unmentionable. I haven't been back there in my mind, not into the two inner chambers anyway, for more years than I care to remember.

There was a time when I could think of nowhere else, live nowhere else, no matter where my body happened to be living. But then, in self-protection I suppose, a curtain came down and all this time since I haven't cared, or dared, to shift it. Now that I finally risk a peep behind the folds, however, the first and almost only thing I see is grey – a wash of grey. Or greys, to be more precise, for there are many of them. There is the warm mouse-belly grey of the château walls for a start, shading into yellow where the lichen blooms, topped by the harsh slatey grey of the tiles on the roof, much darker, much colder, bluer, barely separable from the backdrop of pewter autumn sky. Then there's the wishy-washy lavender colour of the many, many shutters, all silently crying out for a good coat of paint; and the window-boxes, ditto; and the cement basin of the empty goldfish pond, closer to brown in the sludgy part; and the near-black wrought-iron railings with the asphalt of the road behind. Along which the cars pass so close they all but whisk the courtesy title of 'château' away with them, leaving just that of 'house' or 'road-house'. It's hard to think of any upwardly mobile family building their dwelling on this spot unless they went in for highway robbery. The garden is grey too – a dusty platinum hay-grey, legacy of a long dry summer and a lazy gardener who has let things rip. And so is the cat: a dingy pearl. *La vie en gris, Tante Aimée, la vie en gris.*

Goodness, it was difficult to call her aunt. We all found it so, even our first French teacher, Marie-Louise, who was in fact her niece. (By marriage, of course, not by blood, certainly not.) 'Madame' sufficed for the first day or two, while she still stood bedecked, maypole-like, with a few ragged streamers of authority, but they peeled off so fast – came away in our hands with so little tugging – that after the last one fell it seemed natural to pass straight on to 'Aimée' and the second person singular. *Oui, Madame, Non, Madame, 'sais pas, Aimée, fiche-moi la paix.*

And yet we didn't use this intimate form of address. Why not? Simple. For the same reason we didn't stray far from the château, or neglect our lessons, or invite men in without Aimée's knowledge, or commit any other gross infraction of the rules: because her laxity terrified us. Far more than her severity would have done. We were in her hands entirely, five seventeen-year-olds in a foreign country, in a remote spot, in a partially derelict house with a wonky telephone and a whimsical power supply – it behoved us at least to pretend that her hands were strong and capable. Even when they were on the wheel of her perilous Peugeot and we in the passenger seats, being bowled along at breakneck speed to visit some other derelict château in some other equally godforsaken spot. Even when we were feverish and the hands were intent on immersing us willy-nilly into an ice-cold bath. (To make the body react, *mes enfants*. And jeepers, it did.) Even when it was night-time and Brassens was growling away on the gramophone, and the hands touching us weren't hers at all but belonged to . . .

How fast I do go. How fast it all passes in front of me now – a derailed roller coaster tearing by and plunging, plunging, plunging. Where was I? Ah, yes, with the greys, stay with the greys. Well, Aimée's wispy unruly hair was grey too, in defiance of the henna mud-packs she applied to it constantly, so there's another nuance to add to the rest (although strictly speaking the very same nuance is there already in the dusty opalescence of the cat's fur).

And the Peugeot was grey, battleship shade, and when she drove it she nearly always wore a baggy greeny-grey cardigan with the sleeves thrown round her neck to ward off her most hated enemies, the *courants d'air*.

My memory's eye searches vainly for colour – perhaps it is frightened of finding it. But anyway, for the moment it finds none, so it can relax: it is the late fifties and it is Existentialist time in France, even for us bumpkin Brits. Christopher, our only male, wears drainpipe jeans and a long black fisherman's jersey. Day in, day out. He's practically an albino, so his hair, though bright, scarcely counts as colour. We four girls wear long black fisherman's jerseys too, and black high-heeled shoes and stockings, with barely a hyphen of skirt in between. And as for make-up, if we can't find sufficiently pallid lipstick and foundation in the local Prisunic we caulk ourselves over with acne-eraser instead. You look pale, *mes petits lapins*, Aimée wails at us at mealtimes and plies us for some reason with radishes – maybe economy, or maybe in the hope their skin tint will migrate to ours.

Radishes are red, yes, radishes are red. The dread colour seeping in at last. And so, at a very different place on the spectrum, is Matty's hair. Mad Matty, batty Matty, our rich Colombian reject, tossed from school to school across the continents like a hot jet-set potato. And so is the Virginia creeper on the wall outside, and so are Marie-Louise's cheeks: crimson

4

red and lobster red, respectively. Stop here. Marie-Louise is highly religious, related in some way to a well-known Jesuit philosopher: she will have no truck with dangerous Left Bank effluvia. Deaf to our pleas for Sartre and Camus, at reading time she sticks stolidly to Claudel, Péguy and the odd chapter from *Le Grand Meaulnes* thrown in as a sop. Someone has told us this last is a must for all self-respecting rebels, but in Marie-Louise's rendering we can't think why.

How can she stomach the atmosphere, this upright young woman in our morally teetering midst? Cynical Christopher, me, Matty, the live-wire Serena and languid Tessa (whose names would have fitted so much better had they been switched) – the five of us presided over by Aimée, the most unstable element of all? Well, she can't, she won't, not for long. Even if the true name of the game eludes her, the Gitanes we all puff on round the clock will eventually choke her out.

Yes, because the inside of the château is grey too, I was forgetting that. Apart from the fact that the shutters are nearly always closed – Aimée typically shuns the glare – a fog of cigarette smoke obscures the furnishings in virtually every room, bathrooms included, constantly swirling and constantly replenished. We smoke like dogs in kennels scratch: from boredom, frustration and pent-up energy we no longer feel we have. I share a bedroom with Tessa and the first thing I see every morning is her beautifully manicured hand – she is fanatical about her hands, they are the only thing she's really prepared to work on – reaching out from under the covers for her lighter and packet of weeds. Rasp, gasp, grunt; Don't look so disapproving, Viola: gotta have a drag to get me started. And then in goes the hand again and up go the covers. So the bedlinen is pretty grey too – from ash and frequent washing.

That's quite enough about colours for the time being, I reckon. What about sounds? Hmmm. Sounds are less problematic. We didn't agree on sounds, as far as I remember, except for Brassens, and you can't have Brassens on the turntable all day, no matter how Existentialist you are: he sears you, burns you out. So as regards sounds I have a medley of Strauss waltzes and Chopin polonaises and Dvořák and Presley and Fats Domino in my ears, with Brassens as a kind of ritornello theme, cropping up in between. Anything else there may have been – voices, birdsong, even the belling of the stags in the forest – is for the moment drowned out by the music, because that was the way it was: music, music, records, records, noise to cover silence.

What *do* we do all day? We don't. We lounge, we smoke, we yawn, we smoke, we stuff ourselves with chocolate from the nearby chocolate factory and smoke again till our mouths fur. We flick through our copy books, drawing little pin-figures on the corners of the pages, trying to portray them in wicked activities. Is this what our parents have sent us here for? If not, then for what? I managed to get out of my convent by making my father laugh: I told him over the telephone in a dramatic voice that life was passing me by. He has countered my move, sly chess-player that he is, by sending me here, where not only is life passing me by but it's passing by unperceived – there is no trace of it here; you can't even feel the air displaced by its passage. All is still. Through the smoke we stare listlessly at the things that surround us: dusty bookshelves, balding Aubusson carpet, battered Louis XVI chairs. It would surprise none of us, I think, if, sitting on one of them, we were to come across a figure in powdered wig and panniers. Caught in a time-warp like we ourselves are, passed by completely – by life, by death, by everything.

II

Prelude to the Dance

It strikes me now that this diet of lethargy Aimée fed us at the beginning may have been part of her strategy, although, with her vagueness and almost total subscription to laissez-faire in most areas, it is hard to think of her as having a strategy. More likely it was just the dictates of the social season: her – what shall I call them? Neighbours? Cronies? Clients? Accomplices? – all being away in Paris till the strains of the huntsman's horn brought them back. Still. Following on the heels of boredom, fear may not only be welcomed, it may actually pass unrecognised for what it is. Something, after all, is happening at last; something breaks in on the scene and your dormant senses tingle at the prospect. What is it? No way of telling, but it's alive and beckoning so let's go with it.

There was only one foretaste of something spicier on our curriculum, or only one sufficiently strong for me to notice, and that was a curious evening, sometime in our second or maybe third week there, when Matty turned up with a pick-up, a young officer she and Christopher had met on the road to Tours. One of the bikes they had been riding had had a puncture, and this guy – I don't remember his name, Aimée just called him dismissively *le p'tit militaire* – had stopped, either immediately taken with Matty or else halted by the traffic light of her hair, and had escorted them both back to the château in his car with their bikes roped to the roof. He was a little swarthy spotty fellow but he snapped his heels together and kissed Aimée's hand, proffering a surname with a 'de' in it, and I think this was what earned him his entrée and his invitation to dinner and the rest. Serena and I notched up a couple of pick-ups too, a little later on, on a shopping expedition: two wondrously beautiful employees of the chocolate factory who you'd think would have suited Aimée's books far better, but, no, the moment she saw them she chased them away like a bulldog – English, not French – and then turned an isolated flare of rage on us. How dare we behave so brazenly? How dare we bring such people into her house? It was a question of caste, you see, and that was a lesson: one of the few canonical ones she ever imparted and one of the very few that stuck. It's not what you do, it's who you do it with.

But Matty's *militaire*, no, he passed muster all right on the strength of a hand-kiss and a syllable. Smarmy little twerp. During dinner nothing particular happened, not that I remember, anyway. Did Aimée seat him to her privileged right? I think she did. I think she chatted mainly to him too, quite a lot, quite graciously; maybe it came as a relief to have someone to talk to, Marie-Louise being such a dead weight, and we being so impeded in our French. I seem to have a picture of her in my mind's archive, smiling at her unlovely guest and grating nutmeg over his plate of Brussels sprouts. At last, someone who shared her tastes. Filling him up with wine, too, pampering him, making him feel at ease.

Did I catch her looking at Matty? No, I didn't. No, she didn't look at Matty, hardly at all. *I* looked at Matty. I know this for sure because I remember noticing how pleased with herself she looked – at having made this conquest, and having the conquest so unexpectedly approved. She was as sleek and wriggly as a retriever that's brought back a pheasant. Or, let's say, a stoat. And I remember how this fact amazed me and shamed me, because, I mean, Matty – OK, she was foreign and had failed her O levels and had to wax her arms, but there was something attractive about her all the same. The bell of red hair was stunning, for one, and her eyelashes were Disney-long, and, oh, various things, various things she had going for her. Not least her fortune. Whereas the *militaire* had nothing. Except acne, and a hideous uniform that made you itch just to look at it, and teeth coated in tartar (visible, I swear, from my place on the other side of the table), and that miserable rag of a prefix. And yet here was Matty wriggling, and here was Aimée smiling, and here was a bottle of wine going round instead of the usual carafe, and here were Marie-Louise's cheeks turning to fuchsia, and Mme Goujon, who did the cooking, swanning in with an emergency pudding when ordinarily we never had puddings, except at weekends. It was embarrassing, it was uncomfortable, it was humiliating. It was downright wrong.

The stage direction of the latter half of the evening – if there was any on Aimée's part, and you can bet there was – was finely done. Afterwards I tried to piece together how it was that the rest of us went to bed so early, leaving Matty and her prize alone together in the salon, but everyone was vague about their reasons, myself included. Was it connivance? Was it disgust? Or did Aimée somehow manage to make us feel it was the right thing for us to do – just to slope off and leave them to it? Somehow, none of us could say. Marie-Louise complained of a headache, that I do remember, and was the first to go. A real headache or a diplomatic headache? No telling. But the others? Which of us left last? And who second last? Or did we all go pretty well together? And where was Aimée and why didn't she stop us? No one said goodnight to her – that came later. So? Where was she? And why were the shutters not shut, when the gardener latched them up every evening like a prison warder, punctually, at half past five, and they were never open that wide anyway? Why? Or had they been shut and had someone then opened them later?

It was Serena who called us, Tessa and myself; we were asleep already. And it was Christopher who had called Serena. But who called Christopher? No one, according to him: he just heard noises and went to investigate. First inside, and then, in a moment of great inspiration, out. But who made the noises? The snoggers themselves, or Aimée, or someone else, and if so, who?

It was quite an eyeful. With the three sets of French windows ablaze with light, and the sofa placed parallel to the bookcase at the back of the room, the scene was like the stage of a theatre at which we had a private box. A programme of Feydeau with a pinch of porn. We crept across the gravel in our pyjamas, already clutching our stomachs with giggles and excitement – there was no one else around then, I'm sure (unless you count the cat, Aimée's familiar, which was sitting in front of the furthest window, licking its loathsome paws) – and settled ourselves in the shadows on either side of the first window, just outside the trapezoid of light. Serena had mimed the scene for us already, to put us in the party mood: You must *see* this, she implored as she dragged us protesting from our slumbers. You have to *see* it. Oh my God, oh my God, it's so incredible, and she's got her period too.

It wasn't incredible, that wasn't the right word at all, but it was riveting, mesmerising entertainment, impossible to forgo. On the sofa, on his back, lay the soldier, his itchy jacket discarded, his shirt rucked up to armhole level, his trousers down to knee, revealing a white cotton vest and underpants, separated in their turn by an interesting gap of pallid, slightly freckly flesh. We could only see a sectional side view of him because on top, closing him like a sandwich filling between her and the cushions, lay Matty.

I say, lay, but her position was more of a crouch. I had no idea at the time that real-life sex was so ungainly. That was part of the fascination, I think: the sheer absurdity, both of the act and the performers. It was what held us there, what permitted us to go on watching. Had the spectacle been pretty, we would have been ashamed because our prurience would have had no cover, but as it was we could go on gaping and giggling ad libitum. (And ad nauseam, because it caused a mixture of both.)

Matty's bum was perched much higher than the rest of her body, taking on a kind of airborne, independent look. Stealing the show, as far as we were concerned. The *militaire* was working on it, blind, with his visible hand, trying to negotiate a whole interconnected web of obstacles which reformed and regrouped the moment he got past one of them. He would pull aside the knickers, for example, managing to lay bare a buttock, and as he did so the girdle surmounting the other buttock would snap back into place. So then he'd lock furiously with the girdle, while the knickers would recover their lost territory. And as if these weren't fronts enough to cover, there was also Matty's skirt to contend with, which kept on coming loose from its rolled-up position at her waist and slithering down over the field of operations like a safety curtain; plus the lining, which did much the same; plus a layer of petticoat, also proving troublesome, being silk; plus the sturdiest obstacle of all: the last-ditch bulwark of her sanitary pad wedged into the crack of her rump. Kapok in those days, and thick cotton net, and anchored firmly in place like a storm-mooring by hooks and loops and a tight elastic belt.

I stole a quick glance at Christopher, embarrassed more on my own account than Matty's by this revelation. Men shouldn't be let in on such things. If she wasn't careful the bloodstained side might show any minute. The *militaire* didn't matter so much because he couldn't actually see the thing, only feel it, but Christopher could. I don't know how Matty could have managed otherwise, given that Tampax was out for us Catholics, but I felt it was a gross betrayal of our sex to flaunt this intimate object in the air, uncaring, like a mandrill its blue stripes.

As if to prove me right, Christopher grimaced back at me and gave a delighted shudder. Aren't they awful? he whispered. Isn't it awful?

It was. And yet it wasn't. We lingered. We looked and went on looking. I hadn't even bothered to put on my dressing gown and the night air was making my teeth chatter, but I couldn't afford to go and fetch it for fear of what I might miss.

There were heavings going on now. Matty's face was red from the rubbings of the *militaire*'s stubble, and her backside was as high as a puppy's when it invites another dog to play. The obstacles seemed to have been overcome, most of them, and it was her hand that was constituting the last. Her hand against the *militaire*'s hand, her strength against his. Fascinating.

Group sex, even if it's only vicarious like this was, binds tighter than a lynching. I felt a great sense of closeness to my co-spies all of a sudden. I couldn't communicate this to either Tessa or Serena by touch because of the window between us, but I laid my head on Christopher's shoulder and he put half his jacket round me to warm me, and together we smiled fondly at the other two, who smiled just as fondly back. Moment of weird tenderness before the giggles took hold again.

It might have been then, I think, that I saw the other figure, standing by the far window where the cat had been, gazing into the room just as we were, feeding on the same spectacle. Or maybe it was a few minutes later, when an owl hooted in the forest, and we all jumped and looked around in fright. Anyway, I was the one who saw it first, and recognised it first, and the only one who realised what it was up to.

Because, at my horrified whisper of, Aimée! It's

Aimée, don't you see? the other three lost their heads entirely. Instead of hearing a cautious call for their attention they took it as an outright warning. Or, worse, as a signal we'd been caught – in the act of watching the act. Christopher, with one of his gawky, crane-like movements, raised his arms in the air, causing the loose half of the jacket to flap free like a wing, and let out a kind of Indian war cry – Wooo, oooh, oooh! – before totally succumbing to laughter. Serena said, Fuck, under her breath but stood her ground, not laughing at all; Tessa fled, leaving a Cinderella slipper on the gravel; and I just blushed over my entire skin surface; I wasn't quite sure why or for whom.

There were rapid cover-up movements inside the room at this point, but I didn't follow them: I was too intent on watching Aimée – trying to read from her expression, as she drew closer, how long she'd been there and whether she was surprised to see us or had known about our presence all along. She too was in her night attire but had had the forethought to don a dressing gown. It was a shabby tartan wool dressing gown, mannish in cut, and underneath you could see the collar of a heavy flannel nightshirt. (Maybe these garments had belonged to her dead husband, maybe she wore them in remembrance?) Her hair, wispier than ever, had been unwound from the knot she usually wore it in by day, and dangled over her shoulder in a loose, thin plait, like a frayed bell-rope. She cut such a forlorn figure, walking towards us, flicking her fingers and smiling slightly – not scolding at all, just shooing us away – that instead of fearing her or despising her, I felt intensely sad on her account.

Allez! Allez dormir! she called out to us softly. We were her good little rabbits, she was not angry with us at all, only with the naughty Matilda and the soldier, and she would deal with them in a moment as they deserved. Matilda was her first South American charge: she would think twice before taking on another one. Hot blood, she added, more softly still, and the smile broadened and took on a mischievous twist at one corner, Hot blood. Little English bunnies were *tout autre chose*. Off with us now, little English bunnies, leave the culprits to her. Goodnight and sweet dreams.

I'm not sure about my compatriot bunnies – we discussed these matters less and less often the grubbier our collective conscience became – but for me, yes, the events of that evening rang in my ears like a prelude, and a puzzling, disquieting one at that. You know the overture to Mozart's *Don Giovanni*? Those hellish opening bars that are swept away so soon you hardly remember hearing them, but which linger with you all the same, affecting all the other music, darkening the gay bits, weighing down the light? Well, that was more or less the effect that that night had on me: it tinged all the normal days that followed with a streak of the bizarre. My mind

17

soon mislaid the cause – it had no knowledge, really, to fix it to: I doubt *voyeur* was in my lexicon yet, let alone *voyeuse*, let alone *respectable middle-aged voyeuse responsible for my education* – but the effect remained.

Boredom returned, innocence (of a rather studied kind) returned: we went back to our fatuous lessons, put on an Anouilh play, pruned Aimée's fruit trees for her and lit a bonfire with the prunings, round which we danced like children, and then stood, with glowing cheeks, roasting chestnuts in the punctured lid of a biscuit tin, presenting an image of wholesomeness that we were the first to try to believe in.

On peut offrir un marron, Tante Aimée?

She smiled and stayed with us and guzzled a whole handful. She liked us in this girl-guide mode. That other evening might never have happened; Matty's trespasses might never have been.

We went on visits to some celebrated châteaux, in a different league from ours. Most of them – and it was practically all we were told about them, certainly all we retained – beginning with a C. At another, a non-C, which had some link with Diane de Poitiers (famous frog tart, so Christopher dismissed her), we sat through a freezing *Son et Lumière*. We read, we smoked ourselves to haddock-point, we fiddled with translations set us by Marie-Louise, doing a bit each so as to spread the load. Tessa trimmed her cuticles tirelessly, Serena made herself a circular skirt under the supervision of Mme Goujon and flounced around in it like an osprey in a cage. Matty penned lovesick messages to the *militaire* in his barracks. Christopher jived alone. And all the while I could feel, as Aimée did behind the wheel of her car, this insidious *courant d'air*, blowing changes our way. Something was riding on it, something new, something different. Trick or treat, impossible to tell.

III

The Dancing Starts

I magine Cassandra saying something on these lines: Cheer up, Trojans, don't ask me how or when but I have a kind of inkling this dreary deadlock is not going to last. Would it have earned her the same status as a prophetess? I doubt it: when issuing a warning, understatement is further off the mark than no statement at all.

Probably a good thing, then, that I kept my premonitions to myself. It must have been early to mid October when the pattern broke. (Although the days swam past us identical as tadpoles, making it hard to give even a vague date. Lounge-about lessons with Marie-Louise till lunchtime; loll-about disc-session afterwards; a few stabs at homework between tea and dinner, and then an orgy of smoke and rock and chocolate to round it all off – even Kant would have had trouble with his time-keeping on a schedule like that.)

The telephone started ringing at breakfast, which in itself was unusual. Aimée hurried out of the room to answer it, her face still blank and doughy from

sleep – it never took on much character till she got
around to pencilling in the eyebrows – and came
back transfigured. Her face full of character now.
Full of mischief again too. Imagine, *petits lapins*,
imagine the good news. The de Vallemberts had
arrived, ten days earlier than planned, and had
asked us over that very afternoon. For tea, a proper
English tea, in our honour. And for cards as well,
and maybe (twinkle, twinkle, little browless eye) a
spot of dancing. Young Hervé de Vallembert, she
seemed to remember from last year's outings, was a
very keen dancer. Château Vallembert was well
worth a visit too, we would see, one of the oldest
châteaux in the region. It had a moat and dated
back to the twelfth century in parts.

So there were outings, plural, regular ones. Ah.
Had been last year and presumably would be this.
Ah. The prospect didn't galvanise us – another
bumpy white-knuckle drive, another moat, another
historic building with the parts that Aimée mentioned almost certainly unconnected to one another:
we were beginning to know what to expect of these
privately owned châteaux – but as departure time
came nearer it set us stirring none the less.

Sabine used to maintain that preparation for a
dance is comparable to what goes on in the back
room of a butcher's shop: the meat for consumption
is sliced and dressed and put in nice little paper
packages, ready for the kitchen. But I hadn't yet
learnt to see things through her fiery Jansenist eyes, I

was still with Tolstoy and Natasha and the thrill of a young girl's first ball, so I remember getting caught up in a frivolous, light-hearted activity that early afternoon. I remember the bathroom and the ubiquitous smoke, compounded by steam from the bath water, and the musky smell of Omy, which was the fashionable bath essence of the time. It came in spherical capsules, if my memory is correct, a bit like outsize cod liver oil pills. Omy balls, Omy balls, sang Christopher, swooping around, trying to avoid being evicted on grounds of gender. He wasn't gay but he had a strong feminine streak in him, or else was stuck in a puppy stage – pre-pubertal – and he liked all the things we liked, and liked to take part in them. Dear Christopher, poor Christopher, I still see him around occasionally in some of the usual haunts but we never talk now – what is there to say?

Well, I suppose I could ask him to refresh this next set of memories for me for a start. See if his have weathered the scouring of time any better than mine. And the scouring of shame as well. It's strange, when the backdrops to most of my early sexual experiences are practically hard-wired into me, so clear and durable is their trace, that all I should have left of these – these *soirées*, these *visites* or whatever Aimée used to call them – is a jumble of images of moats and towers and salons and fountains and mirrors and dusty wooden floors, and a jumble of faintly cheesy-sounding names to go with them, like de Roquefort and du Boursin and de Brie, all crammed higgledy-piggledy into my storage cells, with no way of sorting them out. Maybe it's another defence mechanism like the curtain, or maybe it's a bit of Sabine, lodged fast inside me, marching furiously up and down the way she used to during lesson times when we were inattentive, cuffing the memories on the head one by one and flinging scraps of *argot* at them. *Fous-moi le camp, salaud, tu m'emmerdes, tu m'emmerdes*.

Which one *was* Château Camembert, *pardon*, Vallembert? And which, of the many young men with V-necked sweaters and hedgehog hair and corduroy trousers with stifled erections inside them, was Hervé? Was he the tall, good-looking one with the rather foppish hair that flopped instead of sprouting? No, that was Hervé Someone-else – an Italian name: Minucci, Carlucci – the one Tessa pretended to be keen on when she could be bothered; the one who came to her coming-out dance later and whom she treated like shit and serve him right. (But, no, I'm unkind: our hosts were just as much pawns on Aimée's board as we were.) Was he the lame one, then, the nice one who liked to talk because he didn't like to dance, and didn't dare smooch for fear of rebuff? No, that was Armand, Armand de la Brioche or whatever. So was he perhaps the one with the beautiful eyes, hampered in his advances by the Down's syndrome brother who tagged along behind him everywhere, even on the dance floor, even to the slowest of slows? *Que fais tu?* What are you doing with your hands like that? What are you doing to that girl? Show, show. *Fais voir, fais voir.* No, that was Régis. I remember Régis somewhat more clearly than the others, and I remember his family's château, too, because of the tower with the bolted door and the Mrs Rochester cackle we heard coming from the other side. Another sibling, we surmised, Serena and I, product of inbreeding, sins of the fathers, and doubled up laughing.

Château de Vallembert. Château de Vallembert. The first of the venues and in its unexpectedness the worst. It must be there somewhere and so must its owners and so must the happenings of that late autumn afternoon, blueprint for so many that followed: a chill lemony cup of tea in a room the size of a rugby pitch, some chill lemony conversation with the adults – *Oui, j'habite à Cambridge. Oui, Monsieur*, the seat of the famous University. *Non, Madame*, the Cambridge accent is not all that fancy, it's the Oxford one I think you have in mind – while their gangling scions stood around on the sidelines, sizing us up, making their choices; and then the tumbling over ourselves as, released, we raced through flights of similar rooms, aiming for some gramophone-equipped den where the scrum could begin.

Begin but never end, because that was the nature of Aimée's game. At some point – a carefully calculated point, you could be sure, honed to the nanosecond by years of practice – creak would go the door and on would go the lights and there she would be, hands raised in token horror. Pencilled eyebrows too. But beneath them the telltale glitter of her greedy, naughty, lonely eyes. Oh, what were her bunnies up to? Turn her back for a moment and look what happened. No, no, she didn't want to hear any excuses, whose idea it was, who started it, we were all equally to blame. Straight into the car with us, and no more parties until we learned to dance nicely, to nice music, with the lights on.

Cruel? Yes, cruel, slightly, but in a natural way, a bit like dog-fighting only without the violence. Put them in a pen together and see what they get up to. My brief against Aimée has nothing to do, really, with this teasing little hobby of hers. Despite Sabine's lambastings. After all, we enjoyed it too, didn't we? Our blood hummed just as fast as Aimée's did, the rushes of unsated yearning swirling through it were every bit as sweet. Nobody but nature forced us to tart ourselves up punctually every weekend, Friday after Friday and Saturday after Saturday, and pile into the Peugeot and make for another trysting place and start all over again. And stop all over again, and start and stop, and start and stop, until not only our knickers, but, Christ, every fibre of our clothing, and of our bodies too for that matter, were in a twist. Years later I saw a film – poignantly sad, and for me unbearably so – about a scientist who had invented a kind of total sense recorder, not just video but audio and smellio and touchio and the rest, which he set to play every afternoon in a given place at a given time, for as long as the mechanism lasted. The scene he projected was that of a dozen or so young couples dancing on a terrace in the same holiday house, on the same island, where the recorder itself was kept. Then this young man comes across it while it is playing and at first is convinced he is watching a real occurrence: he sees this beautiful girl, in her slinky 1930s outfit, dancing and laughing and chattering with her friends, and he falls in love with her on the spot. Second day, second time around, he comes to the island at a slightly different time so he sees a slightly different excerpt, and still doesn't twig and falls deeper in love. And so on and so forth for various days until he happens on a duplicate bit and realises something is wrong. But by then, of course, he is irretrievably hooked. So what does he do? He digs out the machine, fiddles with its insides until he has grasped its workings, and then sets it up in recording mode and records himself into the scene in a desperate last-ditch attempt to join the dancers. Which works, and there he stays: trapped there amongst them in a virtual dimension, forever young, forever re-enacting the same little loop of life, over and over.

In her *voyeuse* guise, Aimée reminds me of this melancholy young man. How many times, and for how many years, must she have watched the same short take repeat itself, with only the most minor of minor variants? It is depressing merely to hazard a guess. Though the music, I suppose, must have changed a bit – the music and the clothes. Young couples dancing, clinging to one another, swaying to the beat almost imperceptibly, their feet hardly moving, while on the microscopic scale their bodies whirl. The males maybe a little more groggy than the females when the lights go on, but not necessarily so. And how many stills has she got in her mental album of a roomful of bemused, embarrassed *interruptus* faces and blinking eyes and mussed-up hair? (Which also must have changed a bit in style before reaching the Juliette Greco theatre-curtains that we strove to achieve.) And how long and how badly must she have yearned for her face to be one of them again? What iron-bound impulse drove her to the gaming board, time after time, to set out her compliant pieces? Bad Aimée but in this respect poor Aimée: for her there was no time machine, no recorder, total or otherwise, no way, except by proxy, of worming herself once more into the scene.

And yet she had no resentment against us for being young, that was one endearing thing about her. Even when, after the hunt, I returned her beautiful costume stained with underarm sweat marks, all she said was, *Ah, jeunesse*, with a sigh. She liked her bunnies, she truly did. She cared for us, and for me and Christopher in particular. Naturally

27

she had her reasons. But I think in this case reasons and inclinations went together. There were plenty of grander pupils she could have boasted about – judging from the photos on the clapped-out grand piano, the cream of the British shires, from the Cornish and Devonshire variety to the Highland, had poured through her establishment at one time or another, and even among the present bunch Tessa was an Hon, and Matty had a brother who claimed to be screwing Princess Alexandra – but no, whatever praise Aimée chose to utter, and whoever she chose to utter it to, it was nearly always us, Viola and Christopher, she pinned it on. Viola the eclectic and Christopher the droll. Christopher the pragmatist and Viola the dreamer – maybe, *on ne sait jamais,* the one-day poet. Just look at this little bit of Lamartine she has translated, and without the dictionary too. And just look at Christopher doing his de Gaulle imitation, *Oh, le méchant,* where did he find that hat? He would never have taken it from the de la Gruyère's hat stand, would he? *Would* he? Perhaps she had better ring the general and check.

I have a suspicion that her stopwatch calculations were based on the exact state of Christopher's and my entwinements rather than those of the others. Which boiled down to mine really, because Christopher hardly ever got entwined at all, there being so few available girls; he just danced around alone, the way he always did, or flopped down beside the gramophone and scanned through the records by the light of his cigarette. I have no proof of this of course, and, as I said, we spoke to one another less and less the longer the gaming continued, but I know for a fact – from the way they fumbled with handkerchiefs and things – that Matty and Serena and partners sometimes managed to go a bit further than Aimée would have sanctioned, had she noticed; and I know that Tessa, who was slow in everything, often complained, vice versa, that her partners never got going at all. Whereas with me the interruption always came at that exact moment when desire was at its keenest: when all was still in the head zone – eyes and mouth and nothing further – and the rest of the body, sprung tight as a golf ball, was crying out for some kind – any kind – of release action. Touch me here, touch me there, Guillaume or Guy or Geffroy or whatever your name is, I beg, I beg.

Chance? Deliberate malice aimed at me? No, nothing of the kind. I think I was Aimée's hourglass, that is all, her monitoring device. In part for convenience's sake, but mainly on account of the special responsibilities she had towards my father regarding my precious virginity, I think she used me as her timer. I think, as she lurked there in the shadows, getting whatever surrogate kicks came her way, I was the one she kept her chary little eye on. What is Viola's partner up to? Kissing her neck still? *Bon*, then we can wait a little while. And where are

29

his hands? Ah, there they are, pressing her to him, linked behind her back. Wait a moment, is the left one perhaps sliding downwards a bit, edging its way towards the buttock? Well, buttocks are on the safe side, let it slide. (Oh, this music, how can young people nowadays stand it so loud?) And now? Now where is the hand going? Ah, where indeed? Now I can't see it any more. What a pity, *quel dommage,* that means we must call a halt to things for this evening: hidden hands are busy hands. Now where's that *sacré* light switch . . . ?

Was that the reason, Aimée? Was that how it was? Have I figured it out at last? I reckon I have. Bit late in the day, OK, but I reckon I figured most things out in the end. What do you say, eh, you evil old sprite?

IV

Sabine

Sabine's arrival among us is another thing I don't remember with the clarity I'd like. The first image of her that ever hit my retina, for example. I'd love to have conserved that because then I could use it as a cardiologist does a base scan: hold it up to the light and check it against later images, and measure, from the changes in the way I see her, the day-by-day changing of my heart. How long, for example, did it take me to register that rare contrast between the darkness of her brows and eyelashes and the blondeness of her hair? A week? Less? More? And the honey-coloured bloom on her skin – how long for that to strike me? And the smoothness of the skin itself? And the long tanned legs, and the wide straight shoulders, and the graceful neck with its deep salt cellars at the base, and the little hollow in the middle that I've never known the name of? How long? How long? And how long before that hollow began to captivate me, before I began to have a secret urge to touch it, just briefly, just lightly, maybe without her even noticing?

Sadly, though, there is no first image of Sabine, and the second and third and so on are missing in consequence, so I shall never be able to chronicle precisely my growing awareness of her presence. She just emerged at some point out of the smoke. (Much of it contributed by her, since in the Gitanes stakes she beat us all, even Tessa; small wonder the visibility was bad.) But if the missing picture should ever turn up, with its missing caption underneath, probably what it would show is a shapeless, ageless, sexless figure, not so much dressed as covered in a slightly conventy garb – navy-blue pleated skirt, white shirt, navy-blue cardigan – and the caption would say simply: 'Grumpy butch French frump'. Such was my perceptive flair.

However, I remember Marie-Louise's departure, which was the cause of Sabine's coming, because it was the evening of the stag party. Not to be confused with the other kind of stag party, definitely not, because, far from being an all-male gathering, that evening several French girls joined our ranks as well, including Marie-Louise herself, bringing the female component up to at least nine if not more. Unlike the dance parties, the outing was for some curious reason considered by Aimée's circle to be safe and *comme il faut*, indeed instructive and singular and not to be missed.

When do stags bell, or roar, or whatever it is they do in the breeding season? Can it possibly be late autumn? I just can't credit it somehow, late autumn is surely an off season for reproduction among all dignified mammals, I think the whole thing was a hoax. *Allons écouter bramer les cerfs*. One of the boys made it up as a ruse to get beyond the range of the light switch, I bet, and no one thought to question him. And the ruse worked, it was a right bacchanal: plenty of *braming* to be heard but none of it from the deer as far as I could tell.

Perhaps, though, looking back on it, we afforded rather a pretty spectacle: the night, the forest, the pairs of young people sloping off into the undergrowth in search of a – what would be the word for it? – a bower, a glade, a clearing, and, once they had found it, spreading out their overcoats and tangling there together on the ground. Perhaps Aimée's prurience had an aesthetic side to it, which was gratified each time her searching torch picked out a couple. Unfettered now by the moral pickiness that made me scoff at Matty and her soldier, I can visualise the scene as not unlike the set of a Shakespeare play.

My Orsino was no great performer, nor his Viola for that matter, but in the dark (a favourite saying of Aimée's, this, and she should know) all cats are grey. His name was Aymar and he had the cleanest breath I have ever tasted. He must have been very young, and very unenterprising too, as all he did, and all we did together, was kiss and groan and slaver for the best part of an hour. Beyond unbuttoning my coat and running his finger round the outline of my bra through my jersey in a rueful way, he didn't even engage with my clothing at all. Matty drew Michel – one of the older and more sophisticated boys, from a slightly *déclassé* family with no 'de' and a château full of rotting apples – and she and he moved much faster, earning themselves a right blasting from Aimée when her relentless beam swung over them and caught them out.

Probably this was the sticking point as far as Marie-Louise was concerned. Or maybe it was some other racier sideshow that slipped my notice though not hers. Or maybe it was just the overwhelmingly sensual cocktail of the whole: the darkness of the forest, the earthy smells, the sighs, the rustlings, the musk, the putative rutting deer, the pheromones, animal and human, flying around in the air. Who can say? Aggravated no doubt by the fact that other French girls of her class were present too, witnesses of her degradation. I can't believe the other cause for shock could ever have surfaced in her tidy conventional mind, surely not. But anyway, whatever her grounds, that same night, when we got back to the château, she handed in her notice to Aimée. Publicly, dramatically, in front of us all, with tears and shakings that nobody quite liked to acknowledge the justice of, although deep down we must have sympathised, and how. It was her second year as teacher there – if she hated it as much as she said, and disapproved as much as she said, then why hadn't she left before? Why wait till now? And why choose this particular moment, when Aimée was all kindness and seriousness, cosseting us with cups of hot chocolate and asking us rectifying questions about the night's outing: Had we felt the cold too much? She did so hope not. Had we heard the roaring? At least in the distance? Did we realise how unusual that was, what a privilege it was to be in on such a happening? Might it not be a good idea to write something about it for our *devoirs*? And then send it to our parents, maybe, to illustrate for them one of the characteristics of the region?

In the wake of Marie-Louise's outburst we were somewhat stuck for answers. It had brought back to us in force our perplexity and guilt. I remember, in the uneasy silence that followed, scanning downwards from her scrubbed puritanical face with its shiny pink nose and Queen Victoria eyes, to the high and defiantly protruding breasts not far beneath and thinking, not without a stab of spite, that they had been set there by a teasing Fate as ballast. Hmmm, yes, I thought, you can run away from this sex thing that you claim to find so distasteful but it will catch you up in the end because you're taking a lot of it with you. You're thwarted, that's what you are, you're not shocked, you're just envious. And she married shortly afterwards and sent us all triumphant little boxes of sugared almonds in silver wrapping, so perhaps I was right. Napoleonic title, the husband's, was Aimée's disparaging comment as she threw her box into the fire.

For a full week after this setback – or maybe it was only three or four days but the pall of boredom was so heavy that they felt like at least seven – Aimée gave us lessons herself. The paradox of her permissiveness, which worked so well on the behaviour front, was for some reason powerless in the field of study. Under her tuition we did nothing, just gabbled away to each other in English and flicked through fashion magazines, right there in front of her nose, planning out loud our weekend wardrobes. Cussed bunnies, stolid Saxon bunnies, unmoved by the stirring rhythms of Racine. Then finally she announced, relieved, that she had found a helper: a girl from a nearby family who, *malheureusement*, had no experience of teaching whatsoever, but who she was sure – this said with a tiny twist of grimness, like a weak-willed ruler announcing the coming of a Gauleiter – would din a little more into our heads than she could.

And it was thus that, bit by bit, from under the pall and out of the smoke, into our lives came Sabine. On a daily basis at first, bouncing in each morning in a disintegrating Deux Chevaux that shuddered and shed pieces of itself when brought to a stop; and then, a few weeks later, when she moved into one of the guest rooms for convenience, on a more permanent one.

No first picture of her, no, but to my delight I find I have a first recording. A cough and a bark, intermeshed. A barking cough and/or a coughing bark, followed by the single word, *Alors!* as she tears open her teaching book and glowers at us over its pages: Aimée must have warned her we are no picnic. And then a rasping drag on the ever-present cigarette, *Zeeeetttt*. It's not a Gitane, it's a Gauloise, and it comes in a blue packet with . . . With what on it? A winged helmet? Winged victory? Winged horse? Wings anyway, wings. Wings to escape on, wings to take you places, and wings to give you a sweeping vision of how things look when you can set them in perspective: this is what you are, Viola, this is what has been made of you to date, and this is what you could become, if only you managed to cross that obstacle, and that one, and that other one over there, which may look a bit daunting but is in fact only made of plywood. See?

Why is she so truculent? And from the very start, before she has even had time to sort us out as individuals, let alone dislike us? Well, let's see if I can answer that for her. She tried so hard to get me to see things the way she saw them, let's see if she was successful, let's see if I can – hop behind her eyes for a second and survey the scene as she surveyed it. OK, there's the table, with her on the shady side, her back to the windows, and on the other – on the side where the light filters through the slats, chopping all the objects it rests on into smoky stripes – who sits there? A quintet of spoilt foreign brats, that's what. Christopher, thin, silver-blond and giggling, looks like the worst caricature of an

English public school boy you could ever imagine –
as might have been drawn by a Nazi propagandist
attempting to portray the enemy's national decline
and unfitness for warfare. Upper class, yes, but so
upper he topples. And what is he giggling at, the
wimp? Why at her, Sabine: he has the cheek, when
he is prime giggling material himself, to be giggling
at her.

To the left of this sorry creature sits the one they
call Vaïola. (She is referring to me, of course.) How
ugly these English vowels are; the name sounds like
a disease. Not so fair-skinned as the other, not so
Aryan – the propagandist would have used *her* for
quite a different purpose – but every bit as irksome:
a pert and self-enamoured little minx, obviously
rich and obviously pampered or she wouldn't have
all that money to spend on make-up. Why, it's
plastered on so thick you could scrape it off with
a trowel. Bet that she's the ringleader of this cocky
little posse. And bet that on the inside of that head
there's far less to scrape.

The redhead? The redhead ditto with a ven-
geance. What's that she's fiddling with when she
ought to be listening? I do believe it's a pair of
tweezers. She's plucking the hairs off her arms. Off
her *arms*, of all places. Not even legs or face, which
is bad enough, but arms. Holy shit, what pathetic
geisha behaviour – pain in order to please the male;
has no one ever told her she has a right to be hairy if
that's the way she's made? Cough, rasp. Well, I

think I shall tell her, right now, and save her from debasing herself any further. Yes, I shall. And *now* what are they giggling about?

Only two more, thank goodness, don't think I could have dealt with more than five. There's that stunning creature stretched out over there at the far end – the only one who isn't giggling but that's because she's half asleep. Another geisha, you can bet, another one whose world revolves around the opposite sex, and who only comes to life when there's testosterone in the offing. The blond boy doesn't really count as male, she looks on him as an honorary female, they all do: and that's probably just what he is, knowing what they get up to in their famous colleges. Doubt if I shall ever get much spark out of her. Fantastic waist, though, you can tell that because she's measuring it now with her hands. Showing off – I'll be darned if her fingers don't touch both ends. What long hands you've got, mademoiselle Tessa. That's settled her. Don't they think of anything but clothes and boys and make-up, these floppy English roses?

And now for number five. The little skinny one with the fidgets and the freckles, what about her? Not such a rose, more of a cactus, but at least she looks a bit more promising. At least she's awake, at least she's got a pen in her hand and a copy book to the ready. Could I see – sorry, what was your name again? Serena? *Quel joli nom* – could I see, then, please, Serena, what you are writing there? More laughter: what do they take me for – a stand-up comedian? Famous English sense of humour at work, I suppose. Well, who cares, it's a job, it's money. And it's *their* money. If they want to spend it sitting round a table all morning, prinking themselves up and giggling and drawing flick-through cartoons the way we used to in kindergarten, that's fine by me. I've got an exam coming up in March, I think I'll do some studying of my own till they've simmered down. Lucky I brought my anatomy books along.

Yes, I can see through Sabine's eyes here all right. (Or at least illude myself I can, because even though I place myself directly behind her eye sockets, it's always me doing the seeing. Maybe I'm wrong and that wasn't the way she saw us at all, maybe she saw us as glamorous and intimidating, and so woofed at us the way a dog would, to show us her mettle before we showed ours: there were deep layers of shyness inside her under the bluster.) But anyway, illusion or not, I often view things nowadays through her eyes, or try to; it has become a habit, a way of keeping in touch, of not losing her entirely.

Oh, Sabine, Sabine. There's an old Italian folk song I've learnt in my lonely latter years, it's called 'Lu Cardillo' and is about a parlour game young people used to play in lieu of courtship: 'Those times when we were so happy', so it goes, 'if I could bring them back for just one hour . . .' If only I could. An hour would be enough. An hour with my head on the pillow beside yours, foreheads touching, eyes locked with eyes (just the two of us, mind you, minus that sodding cat); an hour to smell the smell of you – garlic and all, I wouldn't mind, no, I wouldn't mind. An hour to press you close the whole length of our bodies and feel the shudder of your laugh. An hour to tell you I'm so glad I knew you. An hour, just an hour. I have time now like hedgehogs have fleas: I can lose it, waste it, squander it, kill it, and there will still be more to follow, but that hour I'll never have. Never. Oh, Sabine.

V

Dressing to Kill

My love too, like Sabine, its begetter, its object and its owner, came out of the smoke, but not slowly, oh no. It didn't loom, it didn't emerge bit by bit the way she did, and then consolidate; it swept into my heart like a back draught, blasting out all the other inmates, live and dead, who had ever lodged there. My nurse, my paternal grandmother who brought me up, my fugitive mother who didn't, even the vast, pervasive figure of my father – out they all went, blowing away, light as ashes, making room for Sabine and only Sabine.

Even the biggest blaze, though, has to start somewhere, with a tiny spark, or arsonists would be out of business. This one had started as a dare. We were nonplussed by Sabine at the outset and we were slightly scared of her. She generated giggles but at the same time she generated respect. The word didn't exist then except to describe temperature, but despite her quirks and her clothes and her complete detachment from everything that set us ticking, we found her cool. Yes, that was it exactly, we found her cool. As a teacher she never wooed us, never threw out hooks of any kind, never even beckoned; she just sat there in front of us, Gauloise clamped between faintly scornful lips (a sneer, or just a smoke grimace?), and set before us, indifferent to our reactions, samples of things she relied on to do the wooing for her. This is Pascal, musing on Cleopatra's nose. This is the Alexandrine hexameter in the hands of someone who can really beat the shit out of it. This is Victor Hugo in a sad, quiet mood, all bombast leached out of him by grief. This is du Bellay's showpiece, this is an exchange from Molière, so funny on the surface yet so mordant it draws blood . . . This is this, this is the other: take it or leave it. But if you leave it I shall know darn well with whom the fault lies . . .

(. . . Just as I know already where the fault for your snogging sessions lies, before I've even seen one for myself. You think I'm weird and unfeminine and out of things, but there you're wrong: I've grown up with most of these boys and, precisely because I'm weird and unfeminine, they talk in front of me like soldiers in a barracks. You wouldn't be so keen on them if you could hear some of the things they say: That one's hot; that one's dopey; that one's a whore; that one's got breasts on her so small they're like mosquito bites. Really, Sabine? Yes, really, Sabine. Oh, I know Aimée's a warped old vulture who's seen no pickings since her husband died in the war, but you don't *have* to provide them for her, do you? Not so readily? Not on such a scale? You could – idea, idea – put a bit more value on yourselves and spend the weekends studying instead. Girls have brains, you know, some of them. Who knows? Maybe you do too.)

She's a roaring lesbian, of course, Christopher told us knowledgeably, round about the fourth morning of lessons.

Somehow none of us girls had realised that. (It was news to me even that lesbians roared. How did they roar, I wondered? Anything like the stags?) We were rather cross that he had got there before us, poaching on what should have been female ground. Oh surely not, we countered, she's just a bit masculine, that's all.

Serena, on the basis of a boarding-school scuffle in which a prefect had tried to assault her under the shower with a toothbrush (Which end? Bristly or smooth? She hadn't had time to notice, silly, and nor would you with your fanny under siege), quickly claimed superior knowledge. It's never the ones who look mannish, she explained, it's the ones that look female but sort of tough – the ones with bulging biceps and no podgy patches at the tops of their thighs, they're the ones you want to watch out for.

Is that *true*? Tessa was sufficiently intrigued to sit bolt upright for a change. I thought it was more the clothes – dinner jackets and cigars and pipes and things, and cropped hair and living in the country and breeding dogs. She pulled up her skirt and pinched at her thighs enquiringly. I haven't got any fat at the top of my . . .

God, we knew nothing. Nobody had ever told us anything. I knew so little I didn't dare contribute to the discussion at all.

But you haven't got any biceps either, dolt.

Nor I have. Tessa sank into reclining pose again, relieved, and the conversation shifted to the practical – how and whether this admittedly shallow pool of information could contribute to a correct reading of Sabine. Had anyone noticed her biceps? Anyone caught a glimpse of her thighs, or would we have to wait till summer when we went bathing?

Ninnies. It was Christopher again. No need to go spying around under Sabine's *jupon mité*, and no need to wait for her to take it off either, it was much more simple: we just had to flirt with her, that's all. Not all together, of course – it'd look odd, like we'd been dosed with Spanish Fly in Mme Goujon's soup – but gradually, one at a time. We flirt with her and we see how she reacts. To whom she reacts. Bet it's Serena, bet it's any of you in fact, but I bet it's not me. Now, who volunteers to go first?

Is that a good pyre for the spark of love to ignite? A quarter disgust, a quarter fear, and the other half bravado? Well, it seems like it is. Like it was. So good that I am tempted to think a fair-sized flame was there already – else why should I have resented Christopher plumping straight away for Serena?

Why Serena, for Christ's sake? Why not me? When you are older, Viola, said my father during one of those charged, maudlin, evening performances that he scripted and directed with such skill, you will learn about love; you will know nothing about it, really, until you are older. No one ever does.

I think it was meant sincerely, but what a falsehood that is. I am older now – quite long in the tooth, as my father mischievously liked to describe himself – and I know nothing about love any more, least of all where to find it. I know about taste, and I know a certain amount about the human body, and I know about allergies and food intolerance, and gardening and armchair tennis, and a little about human nature too. I know about comfort, cars, Mozart operas, cooking, mushrooms, birds of prey, all sorts of things, but any knowledge of love has gone, leaving just a sweet-scented rim of memory in my head, like the slick of Omy essence around the bathtub.

Love is about giving, about caring for the other person's welfare. Love is treating someone, in the Kantian sense, never as a means but as an end in themselves. Love is sacrifice, love is something you work at, something you build like a house or tend like a plant, brick by brick, drop by drop, day by day. Nonsense. Old wives' tales, old husbands' tales. That is affection they are talking about, that is companionship, that is charity, that is tickets for the Cancer Research Ball. You must ask the young if you want to know what love is. Only they are deep enough in it to describe. We older ones have clues and simulacra, we base our judgement, like pathologists do, on the dents and scars and sediments of hearts long kept in formaldehyde. It is the pulsing heart you want to probe: the pulsing, beating, leaping, dipping, fluttering heart of a seventeen-year-old.

Of a seventeen-year-old girl on horseback, in the forecourt of the Château de Vibrey, on a raw December morning – can it be the feast day of Saint Hubert? Some special hunting occasion anyway – as the Marquis de Vibrey's deer hounds pour out of their kennels, a howling hairy river, straining for the chase. Because it was there, or so this leathery old relic inside the specimen jar tells me, that the blaze really took hold.

Aimée was desperate that at least one of us should take part in this equine rally, so loaded with social implications, in her book at any rate. Doesn't any one of you know how to ride a horse? she asked plaintively at lunchtime, and then again at dinner, and at lunch the next day. I thought English children all learned how to ride horses. Isn't *le* fox-hunting your national sport? The Marquis would so appreciate it if someone from the school were to show up at the meet, I know he would. He would even lend us mounts. Viola? Your father comes to Longchamps for the races, and he is a friend of the Marquis too. No? You are sure? Christophair? Matty? *Personne?*

Hunting was not cool, and definitely not Existentialist. Imagine Sartre in a pink coat and breeches, imagine Simone de Beauvoir in bowler hat and veil. Brushing aside these considerations, however, I finally came clean about my riding skills and volunteered when I saw the outfit that Aimée was putting on the line as a special lure for her recalcitrant charges. Her own outfit once upon a more glamorous time. Even Christopher would have looked good in it, although in a manner that might have raised an eyebrow or two among the rest of the field. The coat was not pink but a beautiful dull-green velvet, olive-cum-moss, and the breeches were concealed by a swathe of the same material, which could either be draped sideways across both legs, should the rider be sitting side-saddle, or, in the case of an astride rider, be removed altogether to give sway to the breeches – buff-coloured suede, and skin, skintight. The waist of the jacket was tight-fitted too, before jutting out in a redingote flare, and the fastenings were brocaded froggings which did up, Chinese fashion, on one side. The veil was there – a very finely meshed one – but instead of being attached to the brim of a top hat or bowler, it hung from the two side-horns of a green velvet tricorne, braided round with old-gold braid. This veil went with the skirt, in my opinion, and in Aimée's too, and was regretfully set aside. A shame I insisted on riding *à califourchon* and not in the proper ladies' way: the Marquis would have been charmed to see me in full regalia, but never mind, if that was how things were done in England nowadays . . .

Even in its shorn version I loved myself in this costume the moment I put it on, and I loved myself in it in a different way later, because – well, because it led to what it did. How important is scenography for love? I wonder. Perhaps, despite everything, very. Perhaps, despite everything, it even caused Sabine to fall in love with me on that particular day instead of another, though she would have bitten her tongue out rather than admit it: the costume; the Marquis's peppery little mare, skitting around, farting her rump off; the sharp glittery frosty morning air; the yelping hounds; the yew-lined forecourt with the brooding façade of the château casting its shadow over the jostling mêlée assembled there. The absurd, anachronistic tang of it all – the age-old savage rite, masked with the trappings of an elegant epoch that lay between, and crowned by a modernity that didn't even jar, but merely added the pathos of the real, like the fly in a Flemish still-life. The Marquise's goggles, to shield her contact lenses, brought out for her on a silver tray. The huntsman's state-of-the-art artillery. The tractor in the corner, with the cart for hauling away the carcass. The row of low-slung Citroëns parked outside the gates. And Sabine's rolled-up jeans.

For the lens of Visconti, Sabine would have been dressed like me, only more severely. Black maybe, or midnight blue. Hatless, a white jabot at her throat, her hair tied back in a Jacobean bow. The horse she rode would have been bigger and darker, and she would have sat on it astride while I would have perched on mine sideways, Aimée's velvet skirt spread to best advantage. I don't know which director would have put her in jeans like that, or placed her on a moped, sandwiched between two little kid brothers, one fore, one aft. A neo-realist like Rossellini perhaps, or perhaps the early Louis Malle.

Someone at any rate who knew his visual onions. Set off against the riders in their traditional *chasseur* garb, she looked fantastic – smouldering and chippy, like a slightly more feminine version of James Dean. Or maybe, from the aggressiveness point of view, like a slightly more masculine version of James Dean. Same iconic aura, same swung-dash mouth and rebel glare. Instead of seeming out of place she managed somehow to displace the rest of us. Her brothers, far from glaring, perched there enraptured, goggling appreciatively at everything. (Doubly silly of them when she, their sister, was the only thing there worth goggling at: the only real live person in a museum full of waxworks.) Ten years later she'd have had a placard round her neck saying, Stop the Slaughter, Save the Stags, or something like that, but the stags, poor beasts, were not that high on Sabine's political agenda as yet: they were masculine, after all. Like the brothers she had to cart around with her, and to whose education she must contribute money and, if necessary, subordinate her own. No, it was more caste and gender she was reacting against: the artificial, stick-in-the-mud nature of the social system into which she was born. She was reacting, in a nutshell, against the very tricornes and velvets that I was wearing. And that most of the other flibbertigibbets were wearing too, because the green get-up was the official hunt dress for ladies. Grow up, the lot of you, step into the twentieth century. Take cognisance of your *poules de luxe* status. Sickening, the way the youngest de Vibrey girl, to humour the whim of her kinky old father, is actually riding side-saddle today. Twisted round like a blooming corkscrew. Hymen be blowed, think of what it's doing to her innards, poor wretch, think of the strain on her spine when she goes over the fences.

I was still a novice at grasping what was going through Sabine's mind but, even so, what little I grasped I subscribed to instinctively from that instant onward. From swanking, which was what I had been busy doing before I spotted her, I felt suddenly ashamed. Obsolete, ridiculous, uncouth – a barbarian faced with the evidence of another, more progressive, civilisation. A Scythian eyeing the workmanship on Alexander's chariot, an ancient Briton watching a Roman plumber lay the drains. Where did I belong? On which side of the divide did my inner voice tell me to range myself? With the pack? With the baying hounds and the stomping horses and the blithe, confident band of riders, bobbing out of the courtyard already on a wave of predatory bonhomie? Or with the lone, thoughtful, challenging figure left behind on the moped with the kids? The misfit, the stumbling block, the gadfly.

No question, my place was on the outside, with Sabine. But no question, either, that my new address took some time to filter through to me. I was in the swim that day and might as well go with it. Even Saint Augustine, I seem to remember, took a bit of time over his conversion, hedged a bit, dawdled a bit over his parting with his pagan mistress. So, one last hunt, *ma copine*, if you don't mind, and let it be a good one.

VI

The Hunt

The hunt was not a good one, it was a disappointment, and serve me right. I did the same with childhood – tried to stay there just that little bit longer than I had a right to, and as a result my games went dead on me.

The hunt went dead on me too – not stone-cold dead but steaming dead, like the flayed body of the stag, ready for partition: Mane, Thekel, Uphares. Some critic, comparing French to English poetry, once said that the first is like a well-schooled horse going through its paces, while the second is a horse that bolts and then takes wing. Well, if my brief experience is anything to go by, you could say the same for French hunting. And possibly for their gardens too.

Not that I want to defend blood sports – how could I? From the position I'm in now sport and blood can't even be spoken of in the same breath – but in every hunt I had taken part in thus far, the adrenaline rush had always been sufficient to sweep the mind clean of other considerations. One little quick natural death – what was that when set against the waxing bliss of the pursuit? To merge with another animal, to be a centaur again, to have the acumen of a human and the strength of a horse, and to focus these powers on the attainment of a single, simple goal: to follow the chase, to follow the chase. I had first felt this atavistic rapture as a toddler, my mount attached to my mother's by the umbilical cord of a leading rein, and it had never failed me since, not till this day with the de Vibrey deer hounds.

There was no chase, you see, no call for strength and still less for acumen. Everyone knew from the outset exactly where the stag would make for: the river had been made inaccessible to him, so he would head instead for the only expanse of water at his disposal: a small artificial lake, triangular in shape and trap-like in position, situated in a clearing at the centre of the forest. Once he got there, unless they muffed it badly, his escape would be blocked by the hounds on the hypotenuse and by cliffs of tufa on the other two sides, lowish but too high for him to clear. Leaving the narrow circumference of the huntsman's bullet as the only exit.

Knowing this, what need was there for us ladies to sully our velvet habits in the mire or tear them to shreds leaping over hedges and ditches and other obstacles? And what need for the horses to strain their tendons, or the gentlemen to risk a fall and a return to their Paris offices in Paris plaster? None at all. Naturally, everyone was anxious to show off a bit, do a little cavorting around, sail over a few docile fences (else what was the point in swapping the Citroën for horseback in the first place?), so to this end several long straight avenues had been cut through the forest, each one presenting, to the right, a row of brushwood-covered hurdles about the height of a coffee-table, and to the left, a chequered sward of new-laid tufted grass. The direction of the avenues led inexorably lakewards: all that was missing were the signposts.

Hoppity, hoppity, hop. Over the hurdles we went in a tidy cavalcade and made for the next lot. Those who were less athletically inclined loped along on the grass carpet, parallel to the jumpers, making conversation. A salon in the saddle. A mounted minuet.

Where were the hounds all this leisurely while? Loping through a smaller set of avenues, no doubt. On the sound assumption they knew the measures as well as the riders did. And where was the huntsman? Would he have bothered to go with them? Well, perhaps yes, just in case they took a short cut and ended up in the local butcher's shop before the stag did, but probably no: having seen his pack safely off on the scent, he was cutting comfortably through the forest by his own route. Direct to the place of rendezvous, no coffee-table obstacles for him. Wiping the spit from his horn, maybe, in order to get it to sound – the French hunting horn looked to be an admirably designed spit-trap – or loading his gun in preparation for the *coup de grâce*.

For the kill, to give it its more fitting name, since grace hardly came into the picture. In Suffolk, in Somerset, in Ireland, in all the places I had hunted before, the kill had been an adjunct, significant but at the same time dispensable, like the coda to an already finished and well-rounded piece of music. Here, on the other hand, it was the centrepiece. In its absence our dainty little suite of caprioles would have had no sense at all. Instead of getting things over swiftly, therefore, in a low-key fashion in front of the few spectators who had managed to keep his pace, the huntsman postponed his task until the arrival of the entire field. Piling artifice on artifice, and creating a long interval between grab and strike, which is not a good thing, either for prey or predator. Judges know this. I know it too.

The mare the Marquis had lent me was fast and willing and knew the route by heart, so we were among the first to reach the clearing and I was granted a ringside view of everything that followed. I watched the whippers-in struggle with the hounds, trying to leash the bossier and more obstreperous first so as not to lose control of the rest and spoil the huntsman's timing. I watched the stag, sealed off from the world already by his fear, stand in the shallow water that had betrayed him and observe incuriously his fate approach. I watched the huntsman board a tiny flat-bottomed coracle, armed with a knife and a gun that he kept switching from hand to hand as if undecided about which to use. Or which to use first. I watched him, after a few vain attempts to lasso the stag by the antlers, settle for the gun. Then, with his weapon at the ready, I watched him glance at the Marquis, who nodded, as much as to say, Yes, we are all assembled, go ahead, and I watched the huntsman nod in reply, take aim and fire, and I watched the stag start and buckle and sink into the water with barely another sound.

I felt nothing all this time – why should I, a hunt veteran like myself? No dismay, no repugnance, nothing save the awareness of an empty space inside me – a new space which one day feeling might occupy. Almost as if the stag had snagged my heart with his wide antlers when he fell and made it larger. I was relieved, but in a conventional way, because good marksmanship was a thing to admire and bungling a thing to deprecate, that the huntsman had wielded his gun better than the rope. As yet it went no further than that.

Or did it? The kill signalled a pause, a shift in group behaviour. From silent spectators everyone turned chattery. People dismounted, cigarettes were lit, and backs were courteously turned on the next part of the proceedings: the retrieval and dismemberment of the carcass. Every back, that is, except mine. I don't know why but I went on watching, still in this vacant-minded spirit: no emotion, just a moral question mark or a row of moral dots. I watched the flaying of this prey that had cost us zero skill and effort to capture, and I watched the dismemberment and I watched the dressing. I saw the skin and head and antlers being severed from the body, and the hooves, or slots as they're called in hunting jargon, being struck off neatly at the bone but with little strips of skin left floating, ready for plaiting into trophies later; and I saw the meat parts being removed and piled into the wagon. Then I watched as the offal and leftovers were heaped into a steaming pile and covered with the carpet of the skin, to which the head and antlers remained attached, giving the impression there was another animal – an ugly lumpish one of human manufacture – in place of the graceful natural creature that had stood there so shortly before.

Obscenity is a function of culture – a function in the mathematical sense, I mean, its value changing with that of the variables on which it depends. Once the covering up of the entrails was completed the audience swung round again, almost of one accord, and took up its attentive stance. Cigarettes were stamped out, conversations halted, horses remounted. Butchery was something to avert the eyes from but the next item on the programme was evidently not. It was ceremony again, it was a time-honoured part of the show.

(But does time honour things? Sabine would teach me to ask. How? Why? And if it does, ought it to go on doing so? And for how long?)

The huntsman stepped proudly forward, straddling the stag's neck, or where its neck would have been had it still had one in its clumsy new version, and blew his spit-free horn. The horn blast touched something inside me, some old-fangled switch responsive to its old-fangled sound, and I felt right again. Then, putting away his horn, the huntsman seized the antlers with both hands and whisked the skin aside to reveal the glistening pile of offal. At the very same moment the whippers-in slipped the hounds they had been restraining, and the whole pack surged forward and plunged onto the booty in a tugging, growling, slurping, yelping, struggling, slavering mass.

Fragments of the hounds' meal and the deer's earlier meal flew everywhere. The Marquise, who was standing close by me, prudently replaced her goggles. But not before I'd caught a look of most unladylike relish cross her face: three parts Schadenfreude, one part greed. She gave a slight start when she saw I was observing her and hastily hitched her mouth into a far politer type of smile. Mademoiselle, she confided to me with frosty archness, I shouldn't go spoiling my husband's surprise, but unless I am mistaken I think there is a great honour in store for you in just a little moment. When the trophies are distributed, *vous savez*. (No, I didn't savvy anything, but I bet Aimée did; I bet Sabine was right and she and the Marquis had arranged the whole thing beforehand. That was why she was so keen I should take part in the *chasse*.) If I were you I would dismount now and let my groom here hold your horse for you. Like that you will be free to cross over on foot – she pointed knowledgeably to a knoll on the far side of the canine banqueting floor, where the Marquis and the huntsman were now standing together, sorting through various choice pieces of deer anatomy – to receive your prize. Horses are so silly that way. It's the smell, you know, they don't like it.

Don't they really, *Madame*, well, *à chacun son goût*. My prize, my prize. My trophy. I've still got it somewhere: a hoof, a slot, much smaller and daintier than you'd expect from such a large animal, mounted vertically on a narrow wooden base, up which runs the plait of skin with a nail on the top, and then underneath, on a dull brass plate: *Equipage de Vibrey, Hiver 1958*. I don't recall who was responsible for its curing in the end, but anyway it has lasted well. It bears no exact date, but for those most closely concerned none is needed: for the stag it was his death day and for me the birthday of my love for Sabine. I'm sorry for the stag about this conjunction but that's the way it was.

VII

Free-falling

You'd think I'd never be a romantic again, not after what happened and with the life I lead now. You'd think cynicism would be part of my survival kit. But it's not so. I believe in Cupid's darts and Aristophanes' apples and in Once-in-a-lifetime and Till-death-do-us-part and the whole darn caboosh, because that is the bittersweet fruit of my experience.

I've had other passions since, other affections, other ties, other people who've touched my heart and even those who've messed around with it – I'm human in that respect, we all are, despite the image – but I've never had another love. A child might have filled this empty space, which is why I never had one. No one else to really love, ever, after Sabine.

She was there in the château, sitting in the half-light of the salon correcting homework, when I got back from the hunt, trophy still dangling from my hand. To tell the truth I was at a slight loss as to what to do with this trophy affair. Aimée said there was no taxidermist locally and we'd have to wait until someone going back to Paris was willing to take it for me. The de Vallemberts maybe, or else the Marquis himself: he was always helpful where the needs of a *jolie jeune fille* were concerned. But meanwhile I was stuck with the thing. I felt impeded and ashamed, like a chicken-killing dog whose victim has been hung round its neck as a deterrent to further raids.

So? Sabine said, scarcely bothering to look up from her work. (That fearsome *alors*: capable of acting as goad, gibe or growl, depending. Now it was a growl.) Enjoy yourself, scampering through the woods with all the *beau monde*?

The volume of my 'no' made her check a little and she raised her head and looked at me square.

No?

No.

And that was it more or less. The space of three nos. I looked back every inch as square, and this was when it happened. It was the first occasion, since the start of Christopher's dare, that our eyes had held each other's gaze for any length of time. Up till then it had been grandmother's footsteps: a long hard stare to make the other one look, and when she did – or when I did – a quick turning away before we were caught. Probably we had known all along the effect that prolonged eye contact would have, and probably that was why we had shunned it. Shyness, fear of the thing that would grow into being between us. No, not grow, that would burst into being between us. Because that's what love is, take note all you parched old fogeys with your evolution theories and your gardening theories and your painstaking Lego constructions, block on piddling little block, that's what love is and that's how it's born: fully grown like Minerva. First sight, maybe not, but first look, first real deep look.

And anguish and happiness are born along with it – quite different from the wishy-washy namesakes you have felt before. You suffer a sky change. Your world switches solar systems, a different sun rises on it, shedding a different light: warmer, brighter, more intense. The rose-pink of tradition, no, that's songwriters' shorthand, but neither was it *la vie en gris* any more: it was the dawn of my brief *vie en or*. I had a much loved pet rabbit when I was little to which I gave the most splendid name I could think of: Goldie. Forbearing smile from my father at this childish choice, but I stuck by it and still do: gold is tops and gold is the colour I will for ever associate with Sabine. Gold hairs on her skin, on her arms and the back of her neck, gold streaks in her hair, gold flecks in those true tortoiseshell eyes of hers that could never lie, never conceal anything, not even with the lids shut. And gold light on everything from that moment on. And all the darker the darkness when the light went out.

I had no time to appreciate these great astronomical developments, however, because at this point, to the surprise of us both, Sabine suddenly snatched the hoof from me and lashed its ribbons of skin across my face.

Hey! That hurt! Why did you do that?

I don't know. My hand did it for me. Why did *you* take part in that absurd masquerade? Why did you let Aimée talk you into it? She does it every year – gets one of her pupils to fill the part, wear the costume, act all simpery with the Marquis: '*Moi? Oh, merci, Monsieur.*' 'But not at all, *Mademoiselle,* you deserve it: so plucky, so *capable.*' And all for this . . . this miserable piece of deer flesh that'd have been better left where it was. I bet he called you his *belle amazone anglaise,* eh? That's his usual line. And he generally says it with a leer, too, and a look that goes through all that velvet like it was fishnet. Oh, he gives me the creeps, that man, with his hand-kissing and his phoney Maurice Chevalier smile: Zank Heavens for Leetle Girls. Lucky the son wasn't there today, or he'd probably have invited you to . . .

Jealousy. Oh, jealousy in a partner is wonderful. It wraps round you like a fur coat, warm and protective. And all the time our eyes are having quite a different conversation from the one we speak aloud. Will the two eventually blend? Will we have the guts to blend them? I can't help laughing. Happiness is bubbling up in the bottom of my stomach; it'll come out eventually, like a belch – I shan't be able to control it. She is so fierce, so stern; will she take it amiss?

The son? I ask. I didn't know there was a son. Have we met him yet? Is he one of the snogging group?

You'd know right enough if he was. I'm not sure he isn't worse than the father. Worse because not so bad, if you know what I mean, not so obvious, subtler. Roland. Roland de Vibrey. Everything going for him, everything on a plate since the moment he was born: looks, brains, charm, smarm, the lot. And money like it shouldn't flow with aristocrats. Fountains of the stuff. Waterfalls. I am poor, you know that.

Is it possible that I pay attention only to the last part of what Sabine says? Is it possible that that name passes me by like any other, I who pride myself on my receptive antennae? I'm afraid it is. I hardly hear it, I go straight to the money question.

I am rich. My father is rich. What does that mean?

Nothing. It means you're freer, that's all. I don't object to money, I just object to aristocrats having it, because with them it's been purified by time. The stink's gone off it. They think it's theirs by right. They forget what their ancestors had to do to get it – how many people they bled and pushed around.

That's a pretty grim view. Maybe they earned it.

Yeah. Maybe they won it in a medieval lottery. You've got a lot to learn, little *amazone anglaise*.

OK, Sabine, I think to myself. Grumpy, gold-dusted Sabine who for some weird reason seems to have taken charge of my heart. You're the teacher, no? Go ahead and teach.

You're not one of them, though, are you? she goes on. To begin with I thought you were. Despite the hunt and everything, and those clothes you're wearing and that idiotic boat affair you've got on your head, you're not one of them.

Not one of what?

Not a prisoner. Not a puppet. Not one of those who dance when the dancing master says 'Dance,' and stops when he says 'Stop.' To the music he chooses. Always the same tune, always the same steps. What do you want from life, Viola?

I don't know.

And it is true, I don't. I suddenly realise I haven't a clue. My father wants me to marry. Marry well. With him it is a self-evident goal. The stink-free money that Sabine has just mentioned is the very thing he wants for me. Not so much out of snobbery or greed; it is more that this quick route to power and status fires his romantic imagination. So far I have unquestioningly gone along with this view, but now I know that I don't share it and never have done. So? Where does that leave me? What roads are open to me? Which, if any, beckon? Total fog. I have no road map, no one has ever thought to hand me one.

Sabine's face brightens. You don't know. That's good. That's still more proof you're not one of them. If you were, you would know, you'd have it all clear in your head: success, money, children, friends, luck, health, happiness, comfort, a nice home, a nice car, a clear conscience on the top of it. All the bourgeois idols – all the pretty little porcelain knick-knacks to set out on your shelf. I've got that, I've got that, now all I need is that. And when you've got them . . .

I wouldn't mind being healthy and happy, I tell her, and having lots of friends.

Hah, she scoffs. Nor would I. But there's more to it than that. We should want everything, is my theory, everything there is on offer. Knowledge, knowledge above all of course, but then that's how you get it. By tasting everything, cramming everything into you that you come across. Pain, longing, suffering, fury, humiliation – we've got to learn about these things too, or we seal ourselves off from the rest of humanity in a soap bubble – a perfumed soap bubble. Which is going to burst anyway in the end, so what's the point? You can't grow properly in a soap bubble. You can't breathe. You stay small and damp and stunted and wheezy, and you're so scared of breaking it yourself you hardly dare move. That's not the way to make friends, *ma mignonne*. Nor the way to stay happy and healthy either, nor . . .

Learn about them or experience them?

What?

These things you mentioned. Pain, longing, suffering. Learn *about* them, or experience them?

Tiens, you have a finicky mind, Viola, you could study law with a mind like that. At university too, with proper teachers, instead of just fiddling around like you're doing now . . .

Which: learn about or experience?

She shrugs. I don't know. Whichever it takes, whichever it takes to stay out of the suffocating bourgeois bubble – out of the gas chamber of the soul.

Heavens, she's earnest. And so different from me it makes me boggle. Love is that as well, I was forgetting: it is taking a huge gamble, staking your all on a single improbable throw, jumping off a cliff and trusting an unknown person to catch you before you hit the ground. Myself, I long to live in a bourgeois bubble. With Sabine, and puff cigars if need be and crop my hair and raise Alsatians – there is nothing I'd like better, but I can't tell her that yet. Nor can I tell her that she's all I'll ever want in the way of a teacher. All I can do is go and have my Omy bath and macerate in my good fortune. I'm hurtling downwards fast but so is she: nothing to fear, we'll do a double catch act and sweep each other up in our arms to mutual safety well before we crash.

I have often wondered if any of my skin particles came off during that lashing? I wonder if any are still attached to the stag's, clinging to the plait after all these years? The impact was sharp, it's quite probable a few cells changed places: deer to me, and vice versa. I like this thought: in the end we are all one – prey, predator, victim, aggressor, all one huge jam roll of matter. So it doesn't matter, Viola, doesn't matter . . .

VIII

The Christmas Break

At Christmas we went back to England – all except for Matty who spent the fortnight in Paris with her parents.

I don't remember whether we trained it or flew, or whether we went all four together or separate. I travelled like an object – a fragile object in a packing case, insulated in the wadding of my love. If the others were with me they took care not to interfere with the wrappings. Young people respect each other that way far more than older ones do: it must have been fairly obvious there was what Aimée called *du tendre* between me and Sabine – we neither of us took steps to hide it, why should we? – but there had been no more talk of lesbians in my hearing. Nor had I taken any further part in the smooching sessions, but no one seemed to pay particular attention to this or even notice. Except for Tessa, who was quick to nab my winkle-pickers, seeing as I didn't need them for sitting home reading with Sabine, and Aimée, who viewed this sudden bookish turn of mine with her usual weird relish for all things innocent. *Charmant* to see two young girls bent over their studies. The de Reblochon boys would miss us, they had arranged a firework display, but there, culture must come before fireworks. Now, look after the cat, please, let it in if it wants, and into the Peugeot with the rest . . . (Let the cat in? Old hoodwinker, she knew darn well it couldn't come back till she did. Or could it? That was one little detail I never really fully worked out.) In fascist Italy, said Sabine in a musing voice as the car drove off, they used to have travelling brothels. Wonder if that's where she got the idea from?

My father, although it costs me to admit it, was still close to me at that time; close enough at least to feel – with his nerve-ends, no words needed – that this homecoming daughter was somewhat different from the one he'd seen off. Before, I had always responded to his moods, his rhythms, his whimsical timetable, which decreed no life should assert itself in the house until he gave the signal. A stricture that was all the more easy to enforce now that my grandmother was dead. She used to have blitzes: tea parties, unannounced visits, mornings of pot-pourri making or sloe-gin brewing, events that called for flurry, which would chase my father, grumbling, into his private retreat on the neglected top floor where only the dogs ventured – dogs and dust and spiders. Since her death, however, the whole house had become his retreat, and he had organised its ways accordingly. Cleaning was done silently and early by a bevy of old helper-biddies who had never ceased to adore him. (Save for a brief period when my mother had been around, but they had seen him punished for his fecklessness and had since taken him back into their hearts. He had winning ways with females of all ages, oh yes.) Cooking was done a little later, its smells and noises sealed off behind the barrier of a heavy green baize door through which no one was allowed to pass until lunchtime. Only Miss Marklin, the secretary, and myself were exempted from this rule and could come and go at will, but once on my father's side of the barrier another set of sub-rules came into force. Miss Marklin could sit in the office and work, so long as she did so by the light of her green-shaded desk lamp and didn't use the typewriter: sunshine was bad for hangovers and the tapping of the keys went through the sufferer's head like a weevil. I could do anything I liked if I kept to my bedroom, even play that obnoxious Elvis Presley, but if I wanted to sit around elsewhere and read, for example, or write letters, or do anything that called for daylight, it must be in the summer house, and if I wanted music it must be classical. Strictly classical: no Baroque, no romantic, and no bloody modern. Meaning anything written since Brahms.

Lunch was generally a subdued affair but not always, depending on my father's alcohol intake: if low, he could be as remote and silent as he was at breakfast, and the meal likewise; if high, it could become like a minor version of dinner. Shorter, but dazzling while it lasted. Because dinner was when the lights went on – inside his head as well as out; dinner was a happening, a rite; dinner was when the curtain went up on a world of his creating, and he stepped forward and took you by the hand and whisked you into it.

Often there were guests, sometimes there weren't. I liked the evenings with guests best – they went on longer, they began earlier, with a preparation stage to which, like a trusted prop girl, I was sometimes admitted. Caroline is coming tonight, Viola. You remember Caroline? Teddy's moll. The thin blonde one who models for *Vogue*, who we all got so excited about until we realised it was only hands and legs. Well, tonight I am going to get her to cry. Don't ask me how, when she's tough as they come, but before eleven – no, let's make it harder, let's make it half past ten – I am going to have her in floods. Angry ones, not sad ones, I don't want anyone to be sad except me. You don't believe it's possible? Wait and see. Rosie is coming too. Goody. What shall we do with Rosie? Where shall we put her? And what about old Sir Bas, who she always drags along in her wake? I would like to rattle Sir Bas, oh yes, indeed I would. They say that when he was a diplomat he once drank Mustafa Kemal under the table: what about getting him to show some of his old form tonight? Ply him with the pink gin, lovekin, and we'll have a bash. Remember, always say to him: Would you like a drink, Sir Basil? Never, Would you like another drink? And that applies to everyone.

Obedient, admiring, attentive, conniving – I was no longer any of these things. And not out of pure rebellious spirit, which he might have liked, might have found flattering, but simply because I was often elsewhere in my thoughts. I ate my meals in England, took my baths in England, but that was about it: the rest of the time, save for brief spells when I was in Luxembourg listening to the radio there, I was in France. I read Saint-Simon and de Montherlant – ostentatiously, not taking in much of either. A snob and a loony – my French would have to progress a lot before I would appreciate why Sabine had recommended them. However, for sheer size they served as a good bulwark against my father's soundings.

What's up with you, Viola? You're so silent. Have you fallen for a frog, or what? Don't fall for a frog. They don't wash enough. And oh, that garlic, you can smell it the moment the porters step on the ferry for your luggage: it rolls before them like a bank of dust before bisons. No, I would hate a French son-in-law. Come on, leave those dreary tomes and let's have a game of chess.

Chess, our old sparring ground. I was no match for him but sometimes, flukily, through sheer stubbornness and refusal to quit, I could give him a bit of a battle. Now I just moved the pieces around, wondering inside myself what he would make of a French daughter-in-law.

I'll have your queen if you do that.

Take her then, the silly old trout, I muttered to myself, shoving my bishop to a random square. Let's get it over with.

And if you do that it's check. Where's my old bottle of water/daughter got to, eh? Where's my budding Botvinnik? You may well have learned some French with that Madame Whatshername, but at the expense of half your brain cells by the looks of things.

No, he was wrong, at the expense of my entire being. I was not his bottle of water any more, or his budding Botvinnik or his anything else, and he knew it. Tonight, I vowed silently, I'll leave you to cope alone with your guests and your manoeuvrings and your storm-in-a-wine-glass dramas, I have better things to do. And tomorrow morning I'll fill the house with 'Jailhouse Rock' and sunshine. I am tired of abiding by your cranky rules: if you have morning-after headaches it's your own fault: you shouldn't drink so much.

Or smoke so much either. Cigarettes – another point of contention between us, perhaps the most symbolic of all. Following a shaky theory of my father's that if he actively encouraged me in the habit I would smoke less not more, cigarettes were always strewn around the house, in big help-yourself silver boxes, one to practically every room.

They were his own special brand: a loose-packed tipless cylinder of Virginia tobacco that smelt of molasses, let off a damp blue smoke, and left bitter, treacly flakes on your tongue. During all recent school holidays I had puffed on them avidly (my father tended to keep count of things, fags especially, so I knew the bonanza wouldn't last); now, after the toasty French taste I had become accustomed to, they turned my stomach, made me physically sick. When he pressed one on me I turned away with an Ugh.

He read the signal clearly – I said he was still too close for comfort. Love him, love his cigarettes, and vice versa: shun them, shun him. I was slipping from his grasp. He didn't know how fast and he didn't know why – was it just natural independence asserting itself or was there someone on the other side, pulling? – but his biddable Viola (named for the violin he loved to play and also to bend to his will, insofar as that was possible for a lazy dilettante who could never be bothered to practise) was slipping from his grasp.

Oh, a daughter's education was such a headache in this day and age. What should he do? What could he do? Too late now to send her somewhere else: there weren't many suitable places anyway, and the ones there were got so booked up. Could it be anything seriously to worry about? Could Madame Tiddlypush be unreliable on this score? Surely not, people swore by her. There *had* been an accident once, apparently, but a long time ago and not of that kind . . . something to do with a car. Well, that was one thing at least he needn't worry about, or not until Viola passed her test: car crashes. And even then – lightning never struck twice. All the same, perhaps he ought to have a word with Madame over the blower before the next term started, just to be on the safe side. Tell her to keep her eyes open. How could he put it in his rusty French that would hit the right note and not give offence? *Cherchez l'homme? Gare à qui la touche?* He had lost a wife to an alien plunderer once, he was damned if he was going to lose a daughter.

IX

A Sliver of Bliss

*H*appiness makes for a boring story, so they say.
Well, not to worry, there wasn't much happiness to relate, not lengthwise. The brief Easter term I
went back to, the brief Easter holiday that followed
– miraculously spent staying with Sabine because
my father was away travelling and Aimée was busy
doing I dread to think what – how long would it
have been? Three and a half months? Not much
longer. Bear with me, then, through this blissful/
boring time: the tempo will soon pick up again.

There's not even any sex to tide us over. Just
closeness, and gender-free passion, and two young
girls' minds roving through their private universe
together. A universe made of paper mostly: we read
ourselves blind. Men are so sold on the fucking,
Sabine said, they get drawn into love by it: *foutre*
today, *foutre* tomorrow, and that's it, they're
hooked. With us it will be different: we will be so
sold on the love it will one day draw us into fucking.

As if our time together had no boundary. As if, as
if.

Once, only once, she got me to masturbate in front of her – but in a didactic spirit, to make sure I was doing it properly. It's a point of strength if you can give yourself pleasure, she explained. Like that you don't have to depend on others, don't give them leverage over you. If the clitoris is enough to get you off, as it seems it is with you, then that's fine, the longer you can stay with it the better, but if you find you need some friction on the inside as well, then I suggest fingers to start with. What do you mean, you won't be able to manage it? Of course you'll be able to manage it. Two hands can do two different things at once, don't be feeble. Try now. Try rubbing your head and patting your stomach at the same time. See? That's all it takes – a bit of concentration, a bit of practice, and you're away. If you do graduate to objects, though, remember: never use anything composite or difficult to retrieve. My medical books are full of lists of items that have got marooned up people's bodies by mistake. Yes, even a portable umbrella cover, I swear. Although heading the list are Johnny Walker corks, but why Johnny Walker I have no idea, perhaps the name makes it a shade more personal. I de-virginised myself with a courgette, but that wasn't very clever either.

Oh, yes, Sabine, it was; if only I had followed your example. In the void I shout out your name sometimes. The world is so weird, with its black holes and time worms, perhaps in some dimension you can hear me. (The same way I can hear you now. That's right, *Coeur de lion*, you are saying: Shift to mysto-physics when all else fails. Perhaps in some dimension I am still there, eating and grousing and puffing on my reefers. Hah. Little tip: perhaps you ought to go and see a good psychiatrist – regularly, I mean, undertake a proper course of therapy – before it's too late. Coming up to retirement age and you're still raving on about that cat and the blood and the Marquise . . .)

And, oh, you too, my loved and hated father. I shout yours too. No, I don't blame you for what you did – you were doing your best for me, I know, on your scale of values: getting me into the right set, assuring me a dim and lasting future – I blame you for what you *didn't* do. I blame you for your silence. And for the veils and curtains you drew over everything, as far back as I remember. You weren't shielding me, you know, you were exposing me. The half-light, the half-said, the dreadful bog of ignorance in which you left me floundering – this is what I blame you for. Oh, I grant the facts of *your* life might have been difficult to expound to a growing child, might even have been impossible, but that's not what I'm talking about here and you know it. I'm talking about my grandmother's – your mother's – deathbed, for one. Why did you let me go into that room of horrors unwarned, unarmed, uninformed? I could have said goodbye to her properly, I could have understood why she couldn't say goodbye to me. I could have governed the grim paraphernalia of the sickroom – those towel-covered basins and stained wads of gauze – so they wouldn't have haunted my head at night-time, drifting around in my dreams like ghostly galleons. Or, if they had, at least I would have been empowered by knowledge to repulse them.

I am talking – yes, I am, yippee, at last one of us is – about my mother's flight as well. Why didn't you give me a scrap of mental armour against that either? For years I thought it was me she had run away from. Didn't that ever occur to you – that in my ignorance I might blame myself and suffer as a result? A child so bad her own mother gives up on her and scarpers – with a ski instructor, of all people, she who doesn't even like skiing. Again, maybe you couldn't have told me everything, or even very much, but you could have told me *something*. Told me that marriages fail one in three, or whatever the statistic is; that young women get restless and hanker after a day-life as well as a night-life. After mountain air as well as the fumes of the Four Hundred, or whatever your favourite hang-out in those days was called. You could have told me about the accident in which she died, too. Yourself, instead of just dousing my bedlinen in your tears and leaving the task to Grandmother. It was beyond you at that moment? OK, fair enough – a steering wheel through the sternum is so neat an end in the circumstances that it almost smacks of purpose – but you could have spoken about it later, spoken about her later. *Spoken*, for Christ's sake . . . If only to say you couldn't speak – for sorrow, if that was what it was, and not just rage at her having given you the slip for good. Knowledge may not be power – Sabine may have been too optimistic on that score – but ignorance is weakness, that's for sure, and with that diet of ignorance you raised me weak and left me weak.

And stayed weak yourself. That flipping fiddle of yours, your gift for music, your knack with animals, your flair for chess – think if you had *studied* these things, gone into them, developed them, think how much richer . . .

Oh, what's the point in my blathering on like this to a set of faded video clips inside my head? Too late for these things now. You've gone and I miss you, despite everything. Which is a pretty big everything and a pretty big admission. Cagey, though, weren't you, Daddy, even in departure? A letter with instructions on how to die. Big deal. Still nothing on how to live – just a detailed, step-by-step info sheet on how to damn well die. Big, big deal.

But anyway, no doubt it will come in useful some day. Meanwhile back to France and Easter and my sliver of bliss. So thin I could tell it in a sentence, and so intense I could never really tell it in a lifetime. Sabine's home, for a start. On the surface another of the many châteaux-crumbles Aimée had lugged us to in her mobile Peugeot brothel: the same big, empty, draughty rooms with the little archipelagos of furniture dotted around them: a gilt and crystal table with a photograph of Sabine's deceased father in company of the Comte de Paris (not, as I took him to be, much to Sabine's delight, the Emperor of Japan); a set of beautiful rosewood chairs my father would have given one of his much prized eye-teeth for, with the seat-stuffing coming out; a faded wall tapestry of a deer hunt – typical, this; an ormolu clock. The usual tokens of grace and the fall therefrom. Nothing particular to mark it off from the many other similar dwellings we had visited, there was even a room given over to the ever-present apples. But not one of them was rotting, and in that lay the difference. That, and the bright, sunny, almost magical presence of Ghislaine, Sabine's mum. The place lived. With no money but no fuss either she somehow held it together. No dust, no dirt, no neglect. No veils drawn over horrors because no horrors to draw them over, which to me was the most important point of all. One bathroom only in working order, but a really nice one, with an old-fashioned dappled rocking horse to put the towels on and huge bowls of dried honesty placed in strategic spots to cover up the stains. And even they were scrubbed clean, and painted over, the bigger ones, to make them look like frescoes.

Beauty struggling against privation, and managing somehow to come out victorious.

The mistress of the house was the same: welcoming, open, time-scarred and triumphantly beautiful. Old-fashioned, yes, conventional, yes, but in such a simple, unforced way, you couldn't really wish or imagine her otherwise. Criticism seemed alien to her nature, complaint also. Fate had dealt her no money, a dead husband, two growing sons and an unclassifiable daughter: *suivi*, it had also given her enough love to make the deal worthwhile. Oh, yes, I fell hook line and sinker for Sabine's mum. I suppose not having one of my own left me vulnerable in this respect. With the turmoil that followed I never wrote to thank her for my stay, and this has weighed on me always. I couldn't very well have written later – we were past the politeness patch by then and into territory far more complicated – but I could and should have written at the time. No matter how difficult it is to tell someone adequately that they have given you a glimpse of heaven on earth, I should have tried. I just hope, though perception was not her strong point, that she read my gratitude in my face while I was there. While I sat watching her and Sabine together, for example: mother and daughter the way they should be but seldom are, so close that, although their different outlooks furnish ample sandpaper, there is literally no room for chafing. While Sabine and I lay in bed for four days with gastric flu, and she brought us glasses of barley water, and put eau de cologne compresses on our foreheads, and then sat on a stool between the two beds and read us Dumas. Regression? No, for me it was progress: I was learning what a home was like, what a family was like when it was headed by a brave and generous woman and not by a . . .

And talking of monsters, I don't remember when exactly the cat business started, whether we were still at Sabine's mum's or back in the château already. The picture I have in my mind is simply that of the corner of a bed, on which Sabine and I are lying, with beyond it, at floor level, the rectangular pane of the French window through which the animal is framed – grey fur against the grey paving stone outside – still as a needlework pattern. If I could see the bed cover I would know: clean, and it would be Sabine's home; grubby, and it would be Aimée's. But the foreground is blank, all the focus being turned on that bony, triangular cat face staring through the glass. The school cat, back to its spying tricks. And if I cast around for feelings, all I can recapture is an echo of something distasteful, close to fear or shock. Shock at what, though? At seeing the animal where I do not expect to see it? Or seeing it *how* I do not expect to see it?

Not that it signifies much either way. That cat was so nifty in its comings and goings it could have reached us at the equator, let alone a few kilometres away, which was all the distance that separated the two dwellings. But if we were still at Sabine's, then it must have been towards the very end of my stay, or Aimée would surely have set her forces in motion immediately instead of waiting till we were back in the château for the summer term. The cat shit would have hit the fan that much earlier.

Love was drawing us, you see, as Sabine had predicted: drawing us together on the physical plane as well. The body is its natural medium of transmission, I reckon. Can spirits love? Despite the hype I very much doubt it. And can loving bodies stay apart? Again, unless separated by time or space or chains of some description, I very much doubt it. Sabine and I were coeval and together and as yet unchained – in what other direction could we go except towards each other?

Unnatural? Rot. It was as natural as breathing. Unnatural is the man-made law that decrees it so. Nature makes stags in stag-shape: it takes men to make them in the shape of a stranded jellyfish.

And what does it take to make a nosy old woman in the shape of a nosy old cat? Ah, now you're asking. The cat – sorry about this silly verb, but after that first apparition at the window the cat began to dog us. Every time Sabine and I were alone together, there it would be, watching, unblinking, its head tilted slightly to one side. We even took it on board, more or less, made a threesome with it; allowed it to slip between us as we lay there together, holding hands and touching foreheads and talking ourselves into ever deeper discovery; held it close to us and cuddled it: there is nothing nicer than cat fur on bare skin, or so we thought – despite the grit with which the cat's pelt was dusted, which came off on us like sand. It became a joke, a mascot: our cat. Our companion cat and, yes, to some degree, chaperone cat too, because while it is true that we were young and green and in no hurry, a third party, even if it's only an animal party, puts a break on certain activities – especially when it stares the way that cat did.

Chat-peron. Chat-stité. Chat-grin, chat-grin, as in the fashionable cat book of that time. We never made it, not quite the whole way, or this story would have been different. A Johnny Walker cork, another courgette, perhaps even one of Sabine's nimble fingers, say three to make sure, that's all it would have taken, and we would have been safe – out of their clutches. Talk about butterfly effect: the hymen is not *that* much thicker than a pair of butterfly's wings . . .

Sabine would be furious with me, of course, for clinging to this theory – she was as furious as she could be, even at the time I first explained it to her. They were so devious, you see, so cunning in the way they acted, and she so straightforward, with her logic and her medicine and her science. Perhaps if I had had that cat-fur grit analysed it would have furnished a bit of hard evidence with which to convince her. *Henna*, says the dictionary, *Lawsonia inermis. The crushed leaves thereof, used as a dye, esp. of hair.* Myself, I can dispense with such Scotland Yard procedures: I know this is how things went, I know it – to my cost.

X

The Bal Masqué

Good news, *petits lapins*, I have a proper teacher
for you this term. He is coming tomorrow. His
name is M. Bosse and he used to teach in a big *lycée*
in Touraine. Until his retirement, that is, some years
ago now. (How many, you old slypuss? Come
clean. Like a hundred?) Maybe, just to begin with,
you will find him a little less *sympathique* than
Sabine. But only a little and only to begin with.
Sabine was quite strict with you, too, no? And yet
you came to like her . . .

Aimée dropped this bombshell as lightly as a discarded tissue, without once looking in my direction.
Oh, yes, she was sly all right, they all were. No vetoes,
no tearing us apart, no wedges driven between us; no
hint really, except for the mute scrutiny of the cat, that
anyone had seen any need as yet for our separation.
Just an old new teacher, and an empty feeling in my
stomach, and an empty bedroom, seeing that there
was no point in Sabine staying on now that her
replacement had arrived. Better for her, too, Aimée
added, false and greasy as an old toupee, she will have

more time for her medical studies, a girl of her age, *de bonne famille*, shouldn't really be holding down a full-time job. She will still come in on Thursdays, however, when M. Bosse has his day off, to give you an hour's lesson in the afternoon.

Do you miss her? Tessa asked gently, the first morning we awoke to her absence. What is it like falling for a girl? Is she really a lesbian, like Christopher said? Do you think you are too?

I replied honestly that I didn't know, that it was a label I didn't know how to stick on other people, let alone on myself. Love was such a person-dependent thing: I'd fallen for Sabine, OK, but not necessarily a category or a gender.

Tessa struck up her morning fag and puffed thoughtfully at the ceiling in a volley of tiny smoke rings. Mmm. You liked little thingamajig, little Aymar, a bit, didn't you, too? Perhaps you're both. Bisexual, like a worm.

Yes, perhaps she was right, perhaps I was. Downcast as a worm as well. One hour's lesson a week with Sabine was almost worse than not seeing her at all. We had agreed to telephone each other at regular intervals, but the night before, when I had tried to ring her, there had been a funny interference noise and the line had gone dead on me. Not in itself a major disappointment: dead or alive, the school telephone was a miserable machine you could hardly hear through for the crackle. But worrying all the same.

I know – Tessa was exerting herself to cheer me up, she never usually expressed any ideas in the morning, if indeed later – there's a big fancy dress party at the de Vibreys' this weekend. If Sabine's been invited – and she probably has, or could cadge an invitation anyway – you'll be able to see each other there. She giggled, dispersing the smoke rings. You could even dance together, like we used to do at school. Her leading, you following.

Yes, why not? Or vice versa, seeing that that's the whole beauty of the same-sex relationship in my experience: no fixed roles, no leading and following, no domination. No overdog or underdog, simply an unleashed pair coursing along together side by side. Equals. A draw. Love seventeen and advantage no one.

Does the butcher shop metaphor hold if it is you I am dressing for, Sabine? No, it doesn't and it didn't. I wasn't meat that day, minced or sliced or otherwise, and I didn't cram myself into a tidy package with a view to the customer: I made myself – freely, willingly, autonomously – as pretty as I possibly could for the sheer glee of it, full stop.

On this occasion too I remember the dressing ceremony in the fugged-up bathroom as clearly as if it were yesterday and there had been no fug. Although, seeing as it was the last time in my life that I was ever totally, straightforwardly, unalloyedly happy, it is quite possible I constructed much of the memory in hindsight using pieces of other days –

wishful remembrance and hardly any fact at all. Christopher's voice beating out 'Blueberry Hill' in bad fake American: 'My heart stood steeheel'. He is getting himself into the part. With his hair pomaded into an Elvis crest, and a guitar borrowed from Mme Goujon's teenage son, he is going as a pop singer. Matty in the bath, shaving her legs and cursing herself for having waxed them on a par with the arms: it has made things worse, made the hairs grow inwards and now not even the razor can crop them. *Mierda*. Black stockings is the only answer. But black stockings on an angel . . . ? Too late now to switch to that red affair and go as a Flamenco dancer, it needs sewing. *Mierda, mierda, mierda*. What can she do? Stay starkers and go as the Yeti, Christopher suggests, ducking to avoid a wet sponge. Serena and Tessa squabbling over a filthy starched petticoat, passed around between us so often, as we shift from Greco mode to Bardot, that its ownership record is lost. I have a feeling it is actually mine, brought back from America by my dad, but to say so would only complicate matters at this stage. Besides, it has gone the shape and colour of a rotten cauliflower. Who wants Bardot anyway? Who wants Greco either? Tonight I am to be Cleopatra. I will have no traffic with the musty pile of dressing-up clothes Aimée has put at our disposal – no telling who has worn those tawdry time-stained dresses, and when and where and in what mood. (Why, she did, you idiot. Forties boxes, thirties clingers, twenties sheaths, even second Empire crinolines like as not – she wore them herself, in a mopey mood, all down the decades.) Instead I have settled on a comparatively clean sheet, which I have just finished draping round myself in a sexy Liz Taylor fashion, anchoring it at the top to the struts of Serena's strapless bra and then clamping it in at the waist with a gold chain belt. On my feet I have a pair of sandals, also gold – perhaps more slave than queen, but still – and my arms, neck, head and ears are garnished by all the fake jewellery we have managed to assemble between us – quite a haul. I have a bottle of instant suntan also, nicked by Tessa from a party during the hols, which no one else dares use, and while all these other things are going on I am staring at myself in a soggy little pond of mirror, rubbed free of steam, to watch the effect develop. At present my blackheads are just getting blacker, but on the last glimpse before we leave I shall be bowled over by my own appearance: two kohl-rimmed elfin eyes in a shining brown face, ringed around by curls and glitter. Never before have I been so bewitching. Hindsight, like I said, is a great fudger of memories, but I think even then, at the very moment that I gasp and wonder, I have a kind of presentiment that never will I be so again; that tonight, come later what may in the way of poise and better dress sense, I peak. Not so dire to peak at seventeen. Some do so in their prams, poor things, and some I reckon never peak, they just dip.

This bright halo of confidence came with me to the dance and enveloped me for most of the evening, making it difficult for me to see, outside its radius, what was going on. I noticed Roland de Vibrey at once, of course. It was difficult to miss him. A) because he was standing at the entrance of the ballroom with his parents, greeting the guests as they came in; B) because his greeting to me was particularly flattering, inasmuch as the long eyelashes flickered in surprise and from behind them shot a look of such intensity it had me fancying he fancied me on my merits, silly puffed-up coot that I was; C) because he was wearing a long blond straw wig with flowers in it to crown his Ophelia get-up; and D) because, wig and all, he was the most beautiful creature, male or female, animal or vegetable, I had ever seen. Or anyone had ever seen.

Bit of a wide statement, that, so I will narrow it by adding a 'possibly', and then broaden it again by affirming that the possibility is very remote. Beatrice, Laura, Stella, Helen of Troy, Pasiphae's bull, Adonis, Mr W. H., the Hanging Gardens of Babylon – you can bet none of them had such a head carriage, such high cheekbones, such slanting cobalt-blue eyes with such a lofty *noli me tangere* look in them, or such a shy friendly smile underneath to cancel it out. No, truly, he was magnificent: a human power plant that made the whole place blaze and hum and quiver.

I blazed and hummed myself but mostly on energy of my own generating. Out of sheer honesty I'll admit to a 3 per cent contribution due to the charge of this rogue Ophelia's staggering presence, but no more. After all, what was he to me at that stage? Nothing, not even a person really, let alone a person to worry about, just an extra source of homage. Where homage was due and abundant. It was my evening, or so I still foolishly imagined. I had so many partners and danced so many dances it was like being on a roundabout: no leisure to observe, no time to think, just a whirl of lights and colours and faces spinning round me; and inside, like a pivot holding everything firm, the knowledge that Sabine's face was amongst them, a buccaneer moustache drawn in eye-pencil on her upper lip, and that at some time in the evening – no hurry, no hurry, maybe when they serve supper, maybe later still when the music slows and the costumes wilt and the sidling off begins – we would be together. Strangely, although she must have chosen her pirate guise for its male swagger (I can think of no other reason for her consenting to fancy dress, I had expected the jeans again and a mouth full of Boris Vian spittle), it made her look more feminine. In fact it made her look downright beautiful, like it did Sonya in *War and Peace*. Damn her, damn him, damn Tolstoy, damn everything.

I think it was while I was dancing with the Marquis de Vibrey *père* – what an honour: on the sidelines Aimée was positively purring at this vicarious success, the crafty old feline – that the roundabout gradually ground to a halt and I noticed what had been happening while my back was turning. Roland and Sabine had hitched up and were dancing together. Sabine. Dancing. With a man. And what a man.

Nothing so terrible in this, you may think: the young host and his childhood pal taking a spin together to fill in time while, secretly, both of them would have preferred to be with me. But, oh yes, there was. I knew it at once, long before I knew the reason. It was not so much the way they looked in themselves, although they made a compelling enough pair, the piratess and the drag maiden, both tall, both blond, both moving slightly rigidly to the music as if their rightful place was on a pair of stony Norman tombs, side by stately side for eternity. No, it was the way the rest of the room looked at them: complacent, indulgent, approving. Far from frowning on this unlikely cross-dress match, society was smiling and nodding its head. Next to Aimée I caught sight of Sabine's mum: contentment seemed to fly off her in sparks. At last her darling hoyden daughter was doing something publicly right.

Where is the pain when your pride is wounded? And why do we say that: wounded? There is no gash, no blood, not even a scratch. Which part of us hurts? The brain cells? The neurons? What, for goodness' sake, what? You see, Sabine, not everything is there in your materialist picture of the world – whole chunks of the map are missing.

And how do I always know, a useless split second or so before a bad thing happens, that it is going to happen and will be as bad as bad can be? Answer me that one if you can. I read things into it after? No, I don't, I read them out of it before. His name passed me by on first hearing? OK, so it did, but that was because there was nothing yet in it to hear, no plot, no danger.

The music stopped, we all stopped dancing. The Marquis left me with an ironic little flip on my nose: he could see that my attention was elsewhere, but that didn't bother him – if anything the reverse: things were going according to plan. Sabine left Roland with no particular gesture that I recall and came straight over to me. Her eyes were the same, her smile was the same. Almost. Maybe a trifle wan. She hugged me and ran her finger over the brown on my face. *Incroyable,* she pronounced, it looked amazing and it didn't even come off. Let us go and get something to drink – she was thirsty all of a sudden though she couldn't face food – and then take it somewhere private where we could make plans for next week: how to see each other, where to meet, what to do. She was the same. We were the same. Roland's glitz didn't come off either, she was unsullied by it. Relief.

But short-lived relief. The glitz, no, but the blight, yes. It was already taking hold. It does that sometimes; sometimes the mere nearness is enough, especially when the appetite is strong. Which was, of course, why *her* appetite had left her. I remember noticing the contrast between our skin tones as our arms untwined (for the last time? No, not the very last, but the last unshadowed time, the last time free of care): we could have been of different races, hers had turned so pale. Already, after just one dance. Oh, Sabine, if only I had known. I would have taken you home myself, pillion on a bike, or in my arms if need be, or on foot and dragging you all the way – anyhow, at any cost, to avoid contagion. But it was too soon for me even to suspect. That's the catch of this time-bound world: it's always too soon until it's too late.

They weren't going to run the risk of leaving us *à deux*, not even for the space of a sip of champagne. Before we had time to reach the table where it was being served, here was the Marquis muscling in between us, flanked by his icy Marquise, and here was Aimée, trailing a beaming and unwitting Ghislaine by the hand, and here was the dread Ophelia, wig in hand, his own hair surprisingly dark for a blue-eyed boy, gauze draperies floating. The drag could have been offensive but on him it was disarming. Not so much, 'Look at me, I'm so male I can afford these fripperies,' more, 'I set no great store by gender, you know, it's just the way the chromosomes crumble.'

Eh bien, les voilà, my two little bluestockings.

Having a lovely time, no? Having a lovely time? *Ah, l'ivresse de la danse.* The lights, the music, ah. Aimée flapped round us like a vague old sugary hen, talking nonsense to everyone and no one. The thrill of three de Vibreys at once almost had her moonstruck. (Unless it was all part of the script for her to act like this, in her usual devious-dotty way. But I don't think so: they can't have foreseen how quickly the blight would take effect, they can't have scripted everything.) What a delightful evening, *chère Madame de Vibrey. Cher Monsieur,* so nice to see the ballroom in use again, why, I haven't seen it looking so beautiful since . . . (Oops, that's right, better not say.) Ghislaine, congratulations on your charming daughter. *Si intelligente,* such an inspired teacher for her age . . . such original reading choices . . . Baudelaire, I never even knew he kept a diary . . . Everyone so fond . . . We shall miss her so. And tonight so very *séduisante* in her – what is it, her outfit? Brigand? Corsair, ah, corsair. But did anyone ever see such a pale-looking . . . What's the matter? *Oh, ma petite! Oh, la pauvre!* Is something wrong? Get a chair for her, someone. Quick, a glass of cold water . . . Ice . . . Cognac . . . Anything . . . Quick . . . *Vite, vite, vite!*

It's heartrending. Had it not been for the jealousy I might still have done something, though I'm not quite sure what. Pushed myself forward, for example, stuck by her, gone with her, refused to be supplanted. But jealousy was there, a minor evil among the bigger ones, doing its sneaky work. I saw Sabine turn from grey-pale to green-pale and sway a little and put out her hand, and Roland step forward like an attentive swain and clasp it, and instead of feeling sorry for her something inside me gave a tiny snap, like a little phial, releasing bitter fluid. Not that I thought she was shamming; I didn't. But I had the impression that she didn't shrink from him either; on the contrary let herself kind of droop in his direction, definitely not in mine.

In a trice they were all over her, the vultures. All four of them, and on a sensitive recipient at such close quarters, four can create quite a toxin. I can see them now, acting in concert, giving one another their cues. *Mais ce n'est rien.* She's coming round already. Just a little fainting spell, that's all. Too much *émotion* – smile, smile and slithery innuendo from the Marquis. Nothing to worry about. No, no, Ghislaine, you must stay. Just a little bit longer, stay. Let Roland take care of her, let him drive her home. You can follow afterwards. Sometimes it is good to leave the young ones to themselves. They make such a handsome pair, no? We thought so ourselves when we saw them on the dance floor. *Tellement beaux, tellement bien assortis.*

Poor Ghislaine, the flattery is too much for her: both de Vibrey parents practically throwing their son into her daughter's arms, or the other way round. And now Roland himself comes forward with that panzer-troop smile that flattens all resistance, canvassing on his own behalf. No, really, he would love to take Sabine home, he'll drive carefully, he promises. Look, he is taking his shoes off right now: safer that way, these once belonged to his grandmother and he's not that accustomed to heels. And Sabine, not showing any enthusiasm exactly, still too dazed for that, but not protesting either, which is a weirdness in itself. Poor trusting Ghislaine, it's the sort of scenario she must have dreamt about since Sabine's birth pretty well, but never dared hope for while awake. What a coup it would be: her daughter, with her funny boyish ways, landing the only really good catch in the region. Silly to entertain the thought at this early stage, it was only a dance and a drive, but sillier still to stand in the way and lose maybe the chance of a lifetime. On what grounds, too? Sabine was basically so strong and healthy. The others were right: it was simply the heat and the excitement. She was looking better already, although still worryingly pale. Very well, then, she would give in to the general pressure, let the two young ones go on ahead, and then follow on in her own car in about ten minutes. Say a quarter of an hour. Or say half, because . . . the night, the stars, the moonlight, and that fetching pirate moustache – odd how pretty it looks . . . *on ne sait jamais*.

Yes, Ghislaine is neutralised by flattery and hope, and I by jealousy and despair. Leaving them an open field.

Oh, I know it's stupid to try and pin down causes in a situation like this. Nothing more poignant and nothing more pointless than dissecting the event into little snippets and saying: There, that was the one I screwed up over, that was where I should have acted differently, that was where it all went wrong, all dogwards from there on. All the same, I can't help it. I have the scene in front of me, chopped up like film footage into so many tiny stills, each one slightly further ahead in time than the last. Closer and closer to the disaster point, which I can never see but can imagine all too well. Ghislaine stepping hesitantly forward with her hand bent at the wrist, as if she's having second thoughts and wants to check Sabine's forehead for fever. Aimée catching the hand and drawing her back, chattering her head off to distract her. The Marquise fiddling around in a little beaded sachet of a handbag for the keys to the car, and then holding them up and twiddling them. The darts of light from the overhead chandelier bouncing off the keys and playing over Sabine's face, picking out little beads of sweat. *Émotion* or just exertion? Curse her for either, curse her for both, for feeling *émotion* on Roland's account, and for dancing with him in the first place. I danced with other partners too but it was different; I was waiting for her. She was not waiting for me, anything but. Look at her, the traitress, she has put her hand in his without sparing me a glance and is drifting away from me like a sleepwalker. All that talk about power and self-reliance, and the first presentable man who shows any interest in her: Oh la la, a fainting fit and the vapours. Let her go, let her go and neck in the car with the pantomime dame, because that, now I see him in close-up, is what he looks like. The principal boy and the dame, that is what they both look like and good luck to them.

It all flashes by so quickly – frame after frame. Their backs now are what I see, growing smaller and less distinct as they cross the ballroom, hand in clasping hand, and fuse with the other guests. Their costumes fuse too, until I'm no longer sure it's them my tear-blurred eyes are following or a shepherdess and a cossack, a ghost and a musketeer . . .

Gone now. Gone Sabine, and gone the last chance of saving her. The real Cleopatra would never have let herself be filched of a lover in this way, you can bet your eyeballs. She would have rolled herself into the foot-mat of the car and stowed herself away in the back seat and leaped out at the crucial moment to reclaim her own. She had southern passion, she was a hair-tearer. The fake one, which is me, just has stuffy wounded Nordic pride. I toss my hair instead of tearing it, to show the world at large, and Aimée and company in particular, how little I care, and spin round in search of another partner. Four can play at this game.

The last image, as I am whisked away by God-knows-who, is that of Roland's two discarded satin shoes, lying on the parquet floor. Still life with pumps. What whopping feet his grandmother must have had.

XI

Illness

Post-haemorrhagic Anaemias – 3: Chlorosis

Post-haemorrhagic anaemias, as we have seen above, can conveniently be divided into two basic categories: acute and chronic. **Chlorosis**, also called the chlorotic syndrome, or chlorotic anaemia, is generally regarded as belonging to the latter category. However, rare cases have been described of such severity that some recent authors (*see* Sharnack, Horwath and Thibault) have preferred to place them in the former, under the differential name of **acute chlorosis**, or acute chlorotic syndrome, or acute chlorotic anaemia.

Stuff Sharnack, Horwath and Thibault, says Sabine with all the force she can muster – not a great deal nowadays – and bids me go on reading.

Definition: The term chlorosis (from the Greek χλωρός, meaning green) indicates a particular dystropho-regulatory syndrome, composed of disorders in the psychic, neuro-vegetative and endocrinological systems, combined with haematic and vascular alterations, exclusively affecting young women at or around the age of puberty.

Snort.

The anaemia which the syndrome typically presents is hypochromic, normochilic, non-haemolitic and hyporegenerative, and is characterised by a pallid greenish skin colouring, particularly evident in the face. It is this last to which the syndrome owes its name. (*For further description, see* Van Boorden, Markovich, Robeck, etc.)

She looks in the little mirror she keeps by her bedside and drops it limply on the floor: the green is there OK. Stuff Van Boorden, Markovich and Robeck too.

Symptoms: Besides the anaemia and the greenish pallor, which are the prime symptoms of the disease, the most commonly observed flanking symptoms are: asthenia, anorexia, irregularity in the menstrual cycle, irascibility of temper, virilism . . .

Virilism? *Virilism?* (This really rouses her.) Stuff the lot of them, Dr la Forge first on the list. They can take their virilism and their latinism and their total, total, absolute, irredeemable cretinism and shove them up their rectums. Recti. Recta. Rectis, rectorum, or wherever. They haven't found the cause of the blood loss, they haven't fucking found where I'm fucking bleeding *from*. And until they find out that and put a stop to it, all these iron pills and tonics and things are worse than useless. It's written there, I think, a little further on. Under 'Therapy'. Look, try page 1151. The one with the sexy photographs.

Like her hand, the joke is limp, but at least she

can still make one. I locate the spot she is seeking and read on:

As is the case with all anaemias of this type, the first therapeutic steps must be directed at: 1) locating and arresting the haemorrhage; 2) repairing blood volume; 3) treating the patient for shock and/or collapse; 4) restoring globular volume by means of . . .

Yeah, yeah, I thought so. It's one, see. It's step fucking one. Not two or three or fifty *foutu* five, but one, and they still haven't got round to taking it.

This is the fighting stage, Sabine is in the fighting stage. She is fighting the disease and the diagnosis and the doctors all on the same front, her medical books piled round the bed like a barricade. Dr la Forge has advised Ghislaine to remove them, stealthily, overnight, a volume at a time – there is no patient more tricky, he says, than a first-year medical student – but so far she hasn't had the heart. The books, weighty as they are, seem to be the only thing that is keeping Sabine anchored to the earth. Much of the time she is floating around Lord knows where, light-headed, slow-pulsed, swoony, with her eyes rolling back in her head like marbles; it is agonising to watch her, agonising. But the books with the long complicated words inside them that I barely understand and Ghislaine not at all still have the power to bring her back to us now and again, reeling her in from the clouds like a wayward kite.

She has summoned up enough energy now to take

the volume from me, and is scrabbling through the section labelled 'Etiology'. I'm not quite sure what this is, but I reckon it must be causes. Ectopic pregnancy, she announces with another snort. Well, it can't be that.

I don't know what ectopic means either and have to ask.

Means extra-uterine. Means outside the uterus. Means outside the womb, *bête*. Means the fertilised ovum is in your tubes, up your nostrils, wherever you like but not in the womb. Anyway, it can't be that. Leukaemia neither, or there'd be hypochromia, and the blood test rules that out. A bust vein in the digestive tract, then? Impossible – where would all the blood go? It'd still be around somewhere, causing trouble; at the very least I'd have indigestion and that's one thing I haven't got. What about ulcers? A duodenal, for instance, that somehow they've missed? Oh, it's crazy, if only I could dip my insides in a bowl of water, like the inner chamber of a bicycle tyre, I'd see straight away where the puncture is. *Merde,* this book is heavy . . .

And off she goes again, drifting into her private stratosphere, the effort of concentration has been too much for her. The book slips to the floor, the skin turns ashen, the eyes tilt, the breath comes faster and faster and lighter and lighter – little puppy breaths. Where is she? Where does she go when she wafts away like this? Where is she bound for? Warmth, she needs warmth. Maybe one of Dr la Forge's special emergency injections. This fit looks like it's a bad one. I start rubbing her hands and call urgently for Ghislaine, who is sewing in the next room.

She is beside me in an instant – catapulted by anxiety – and together, silently, we go through our usual routine. Extra blankets, hot-water bottles for the feet (there is a stove in the room with a pan of water on it, kept constantly at the boil). Sal volatile. Under the nose. On the wrists. Prop the feet higher. Chafe the hands, force the blood back into them by friction. Will it back. Will her back. Words are seldom necessary between us in these straits, we share the same thoughts and the same fears and work in tandem as deftly as a trapeze duo, each trusting to the precision of the other's moves.

We don't talk much outside the sickroom either. What is there to say, and in what tone? Cheerfulness rings hollow, sadness rings too full, like a knell. Besides, for all our harmony where nursing is concerned, there is one fundamental thing we disagree on almost to fighting point: him. Yes, Roland. I want him nowhere near Sabine, I want him, basically, in Antarctica, preferably frozen into an iceberg. Although I'd settle for the Arctic as a second choice. I am convinced that his visits are bad for her, and I've actually begun to keep a kind of chart or logbook, noting the visits and seeing if and how far they correspond to the changes in the course of the disease. Already, after only three recorded visits, I am beginning to see a pattern: he comes, she worsens; he stays away, she rallies. The trouble started with him, the night of that gruesome fancy-dress ball, and continues with him: he is its cause and its aggravant. He is noxious, perilous, deadly, the worst news ever reported. But how can I possibly get Ghislaine to accept this, when all she does is smile a forgiving smile and put my judgement down to jealousy? His company seems important to Sabine in some way, Viola, *tu comprends*? Seems to soothe her. When he has been gone a few days she starts to fret so. You have noticed that, no, you must have? Oh, I know it's you she cares for most, and you she wants constantly beside her, but you must understand that too. Can't you be generous? Make a little space for another friend? Do it for Sabine's sake. Tension round the sickbed is the one thing we want to avoid.

I *am* jealous, of course, I'm as green as Sabine almost, and not at all sure that Ghislaine has got it right about the order of her daughter's affections. But she is right enough on the first point: extraordinary, hurtful, inexplicable though it is, Sabine needs Roland's presence, craves it, and pines for it when it is denied her. Ghislaine is right about the tension as well: nothing more excruciating when you are fighting for your life than to have healthy people round you, squabbling over futilities. Who do you love best, and who most do you want with you? Blithering idiots: it's life itself, can't you see?

It's life I love best, and life I want with me. Go hang yourselves, all of you, you're only sapping my strength when most I need it. Leave me in peace and let me grapple.

It's strange, so strange, how nearly the whole of this early period of sickness comes back to me now as a happy one. It can't have been, it wasn't, it was anything but, and yet my memory stubbornly goes on telling me that it was. Perhaps, due to the fact that the main setting was Sabine's bedroom, which I shared with her in that magical Easter break, I am kind of blending it in my mind with the other illness – our joint one. Perhaps over the silence I have recorded the sound of Ghislaine's voice reading aloud to us about Milady's perfidy and Athos's devotion. Perhaps instead of medicine I smell the bouquet of spices in the delicious *pain d'épice* and creamy junket that she brought us up at night. Perhaps that is what it is: a mnemonic fakery, a *trompe l'oreille* and *trompe nez* and *trompe mém-oire* that my unconscious mind has devised as a shield. Or maybe it's my daft mother fixation at work again: Sabine in the grip of a deathly disease, OK, and me helpless to save her, but a pair of maternal wings still spread over us both – safety even on the brink of death. Or maybe, simplest of all, it is just because Sabine was still alive and I still innocent and the worst had yet to happen.

My days were so neat, so structured. Anguish must have been there but I didn't let it set foot over the threshold, not so much as a toe. I would wake to the rasp of Tessa's lighter igniting her morning fag. I would lie there for a second, wondering what it was that gave me this sinking feeling in my stomach, and then, without waiting for the answer, I would get up and dress, have my breakfast, sit through whatever lessons were on the schedule, make a note of the homework, grab my books, jump on a bike and be off.

Ghislaine would have food ready for me, but often as not I didn't eat it. Not until I was sure *he* wasn't there to spike my appetite. If he was – though this would usually happen only at weekends – I would wait in Martha meekness for my rival to leave, filling in the time by doing some housework for Ghislaine: cleaning the bathroom for her, for example, or making sandwiches for the boys' tea. Fear had made me humble and patient. Enemy number one was now the disease. It had a presence as solid as that of a person – I think all serious illnesses do. Its comings and goings were even more pressing to keep track of than Roland's. Where was it today? Was it in the corridor, shuffling off a little bit, ashamed at the ravages it had wrought? Or was it in a corner of the room, flexing its muscles for another pounce? Or was it right at the bedside, bent over Sabine already, its sleeves rolled up for work?

One look in Ghislaine's eyes when she came to fetch me from whatever task I was busy with, and I would know the answer. Worry literally altered their colour: sea-green, and the disease had backed off, at least temporarily; pond-green or mud, and it was present and rampant. I wonder what this colour change was due to: perhaps the lids contracted under pressure and let less light in? And I wonder whether mine did the same? Ghislaine, at this stage, would sometimes train back on me the same swift but enquiring gaze, as if searching for some knowledge in my eyes that I, their owner, was unaware of possessing.

Later, of course, the day I did have the knowledge and was all too aware of it, I would shun her glance deliberately, to prevent her from reading anything, and thus spare her the extra offence. It's bad enough nursing a desperately sick daughter, you don't need a demented assistant by your side, registering panic at the sight of a stain on a sheet or goggling in horror at skin-punctures. One or two more injections that you can't account for, what does it matter?

It was during a respite in Sabine's illness, while we were washing her hair for her – she longed for clean hair again; after health, I think a shampoo came top of her wish-list – that I first noticed them, these injection marks. Two angry little dark round holes on the side of her neck, just below the hairline.

I pointed them out to Ghislaine, a mute query on my face: the less Sabine knew about worsening signs of her disease the better. It seemed such an odd place to choose for an injection. Painful. Unnecessarily cruel.

Ghislaine looked mystified and shook her head. She mouthed, *Moustique?* at me and looked up at the ceiling, searching for a possible culprit.

I tutted a denial and mouthed back, La Forge.

We were entering another patch of disagreement territory here. Sabine didn't trust Dr la Forge, and I didn't trust him either, not since the day – about a couple of weeks earlier – that Aimée had lined us all up and got him to examine us.

On the face of it, it had been a routine check-up requested, or at any rate agreed to, by our parents. Or so Aimée said, and, in my father's case at least, she was probably telling the truth. This *maladie* of poor Sabine's is so worrying for all of us, I know my little bunnies will understand. (Yeah, what if we are little myxie bunnies, is what you mean.) Dr la Forge assures us it is not catching but, *tout de même* . . . A good, thorough examination, maybe a blood test if there is any doubt, would set all our minds at rest.

Would it? Did it? Like hell it did. I have never much taken to doctors, which is odd in a way, coming from me, and Dr la Forge was no exception. He examined us in the main sitting room, which Aimée had transformed for the occasion into a consulting room by means of one of her ash-grey sheets draped across the versatile sofa that had been the scene of Matty's tussle with the soldier. Aimée also stood in as nurse. I've never liked nurses much either.

Christopher went in first. I went second, Serena third and Matty fourth. Which in fact meant she was the last because Tessa didn't go in at all: her parents had got wind of something serious and were driving over from England especially to collect her and cart her off to Harley Street; they were due to arrive sometime over the next few days. Her looming departure saddened me more than I would have thought possible: it was the beginning of our diaspora. I would even miss the morning fag-fog.

Dr la Forge had one of those homely male faces. A family solicitor's face – epicene, rosy and well-shaven – that you instinctively felt you could rely on. Coming from a man like that, prurience is all the more jarring. Aimée's presence didn't help either: our nudity, our embarrassment, the doctor's sticky little hands running caressingly into all the crannies – you could see she was lapping it all up.

Là, derrière, Viola, she beamed at me when my turn came, pointing to her cherished Venetian screen with the gold-leaf flaking off it like dandruff. Take off your clothes and then come back here and lie down. Yes, yes, all of them, naturally, this is a medical examination. *C'est bien sérieux.*

Why is youth so docile? Inside I was seething with the indignity – we'd been told we were to have a blood test, for goodness' sake; a rolled-up sleeve was surely sufficient for that – but I did exactly as I was told. And, of course, once you're naked, that's it; no one can rebel successfully without at least a loincloth.

Now, legs bent, *c'est ça*, Aimée instructed me, propping my heels on the armrest of the sofa. Wide, a little wider. And she draped a grey towel across my knees, which hung there like a curtain, separating me from my nether parts. All I could see was my chest and ribs, drastically foreshortened like those of Masaccio's laid-out Christ, and then, peering over the curtain, the two adult faces, exchanging glances that I tried hard to read but couldn't.

Dr la Forge's hands scuttled over me like warm-blooded reptiles, probing here and there into my flesh, as if in search of a likely place to burrow. This seems all right. *Bon.* Nothing here. Abdomen quite in order. Good muscle tone; nice clear skin. Now, if Madame would be so good as to just stand aside for a minute – *voilà, merci* – he could have a little listen to the lungs . . .

And now it was his head that intruded on me. First the hands, tap-tap-tapping their brazen way right up to the hummocks of my breasts and over, and then the pink, cologne-smelling head, laid on one side so that the eyes stared right into mine, coming closer and closer. Listening, I suppose, to the tom-tom beat of the fingers, but also looking, looking. Contemplating my shame and relishing it with a connoisseur's relish. I could see a tuft of hair poking out of one of the nostrils: it quivered.

I felt disgust, and tried to show it by turning *my* head to one side. Straight away a scented forefinger flicked out and swivelled it back again, and then hooked one of my eyelids and pulled it downwards. All in one movement. Let us just check for anaemia here. No, no signs at all. Ruby red, a lovely colour.

Did you also check . . . ? Aimée was flapping the towel around to attract the doctor's attention. Once she'd got it she fired off another set of cryptic messages via the pencilled eyebrows. Up and down, up and down, it was a wonder the colour didn't run.

Pas encore. One thing at a time. Dr la Forge stood straight again and gestured to Aimée to take up her earlier nurse's stance. Then, with the divide back in place, he retreated once more behind its cover – totally this time, not even the top of his head showing – and I heard the squeak of rubber as he snapped on what I guessed was a pair of surgical gloves and, without warning, moved his fingers to quite a different spot from those they had so far examined. His touch sent a shock of pleasure through me that I hated myself for feeling. How dare my body react like that to a stimulus from this repulsive man, how dare it? I'm not sure I didn't hear a little chuckle coming from behind the towel. Although, when his head rose again above it, Dr la Forge's expression was professional and blank.

Ici, Madame, all is in perfect order, just as Nature formed it, and I think it wiser to let well alone. No deeper examination, *ce n'est pas le cas*. I will just take a little sample of blood now from the arm – for the tests, you understand – and then our young patient can get dressed again.

It was Aimée now who smiled. Her cat smile, satisfied and serene. If she'd had a few worries on the vigilance front, now they were dispelled. The doctor handed her a thin rubber tube and she tied it tenderly round my arm, watching the vein swell and then stroking it several times with her finger before giving it a little light swab. Don't hurt her now, Doctor, will you, she warned with mock severity (almost everything about her was mock that day, except the smile). This one is a very special pupil. You should see the work she turns in – *exquis*, some of it. *Un vrai talent poétique.*

God, I hope I didn't smile back at the pair of them as they stood over me, draining, in cynically symbolic fashion, my blood. I hope I had that much sense.

I think maybe I did, because at least I thought to check my treatment against that of the others. None of them, it emerged, not even Matty with her sultry Latin temperament, had been subjected to the same humiliation. Christopher had even been allowed to keep his underpants on, lucky bastard; the two girls had been stripped and tapped and prodded, but neither of them had had their private parts examined.

Of course he didn't do a fanny-check, silly, he's not a gynaecologist; only gynaecologists do that. Matty was clued up on this score.

So much for Dr la Forge's medical correctness, then. No, I never trusted him again on the ethical front, and when I saw those two wayward jab-marks on Sabine's neck I didn't trust him any longer on the clinical front either. Why, even a ruddy vampire, I said angrily to myself – and later out loud to Ghislaine, because I found the comparison apt and scathing – would have made a tidier job. Even a ruddy vampire.

XII

Jeu d'Esprit

*H*ow long, after this throwaway remark of mine
regarding vampires, before the idea began to
take shape in my mind? (Shape? Does a fog have
shape? Does the twilight? Does the onset of darkness?) Not long, not long: once the word was out,
the thought had only to trot along behind. A few
days perhaps. Maybe closer on a week. Tessa had
gone already, that I do know, or I would have
retained comments of hers in my memory. Laconic,
funny things that would have stuck fast and made
me smile despite everything. Sadly there are none of
those.

I don't have any comments of Matty's, either,
now I come to look for them. So presumably she
had left by then too and there were just the three of
us: Christopher, Serena and me. Which would make
it slightly over a week, because Tessa's parents came
that same weekend to retrieve their endangered
ewe-lamb, and Matty's came the weekend after,
on the same mission. I remember this succession
of dates clearly because we had a poor/posh lunch

that first Saturday with Lord and Lady Grimthorn, as Christopher aptly twisted their name, and a rich/posh lunch the next with the Canal Grandes (again the name is Christopher's rendering). I remember too how interested we were to see to which pair Aimée would accord greater status. We were all convinced the Grimthorns, as representatives of the *ancien régime*, would win hands down, but it was not so. The peer and peeress were accorded baked leeks and custard; the flashy, dashy Canal Grandes, dripping gold and suntan lotion, got roast duckling in orange sauce and a Saint Honoré with all the frills. Aimée, in her own warped way, moved with the times.

Christopher made plenty of comments, of course, but only in the jokey phase. When he saw things were taking a more serious turn the whole topic started to bore him. Or maybe to embarrass him. Or maybe to do something else to him, I don't know. But, anyway, after a spurt of wild enthusiasm, when he would dance around behind Aimée's chair at mealtimes, for example, miming pouncing movements with a Dracula cloak draped over his shoulders, or else stare her straight in the face and let beetroot soup drip down his chin, he fell totally out of sync, and every time Serena and I got down to discussing the matter in his hearing he would make fangy faces at us instead and drift back to his disc-jockeying. 'Two that gather vampires; dreadful trade.'

Serena was my stay, my fellow vampire-hunter. She entered into the spirit of the thing with a zest, an energy, that endeared her to me like a sister, and that lasted as long as she could relate to me, in that or any other way. I say sister because we were too alike, too competitive with one another, ever to bond as friends: like the projecting pieces of a jigsaw puzzle, our characters, by reason of their similar cuts, could never really lock. (Now why did I go and choose that simile, when I hate jigsaw puzzles? Ah, I know why. And I know why I hate them, too.) But as a temporary task force we made a pretty united pair.

We read books, all sorts of books, from lurid to learned, we mugged up our subject, we bicycled to the public library and scanned through all the volumes we could find, and then we made notes and compared them: it was disheartening what a *court* little *bouillon* our pooled info boiled down to. And most of it we knew already from the Hammer Horrors. And much of it, too, was rot.

- Vampires are the living dead. Oxymorons personified. They find death in a violent manner, and come back to life on the rebound, as it were, on the wings of an energy not yet spent. Hence their thirst for the juice of life: i.e. blood.
- They procure this means of sustenance by sucking it from the necks of their victims (preferably young and svelte human beings, though other,

scruffier animals will do at a pinch) through twin incisions made by their unusually long canine teeth.

- They are not spirits, they are a good deal more corporeal than that, but their bodies, although solid enough to the touch, cast neither shadow nor reflection. By virtue of this semi-concrete state they can pass unimpeded through closed windows and doors, although not through walls.
- They are pallid in complexion, shun the sun, live only by night, and sleep away the daylight hours in coffins containing earth from their native land, usually central Europe. Occasionally, for purposes of rapid travel, they mutate into animal form, generally that of a bat. Thanks to this ability their link to the animal kingdom is particularly close, although only to select species: they can handle wolves and bears like pets, for example, but not the larger felines; rodents but not weasels or ferrets.
- They are super-humanly strong, impervious to wounds, and can be kept at bay – if only briefly – by lashings of garlic and/or by a sacred symbol, such as crucifix, rosary or host, brandished in the face. They can be eliminated only by means of a stake, preferably of hawthorn, driven through the heart. Another useful delaying tactic consists in strewing some fine-grained substance, such as rice or lentils, in their path: their obsession with

numbers obliges them to halt their pursuit while they count the grains.

- Their name derives from the Serbo-Croat *Vampir*, meaning an unscrupulous speculator, a usurer, a money-lender.
- The vampire of popular imagination is elegant, languid, old-fashioned in taste and habits, and of bourgeois, even aristocratic, standing, but such characteristics need not be taken as defining. In all likelihood the view is traceable to influential writers of the past, such as Voltaire and Marx, both of whom identified vampires with the richer classes, battening on to the poor for gain.
- The first officially recorded case dates back to 1725: one Andreas Berge crops up in the parish register of Barnin in Moravia as being missing from the grave, his corpse '*vampertione infecta*'.

And that was it: our handbook, our state-of-the-art compendium. All that we could garner in the way of knowledge to help us in our Spot-the-Vampire quest. Not exactly encyclopaedic in scope, but it enabled us to pick out our three main suspects immediately, merely by scanning through the above points and ticking off, against their names, those that applied.

Christopher was still with us at that stage – in spirit, I mean, as well as body. It was he who did the ticking. And most of the talking too.

I'm with Viola on this: Roland is one, you can bet

your last lei. Odd, how we never rumbled him before. Posh and pale, and spooky as they come, and now guzzling himself silly on poor Sabine's blood – that's four points, straight off. And talk about old-fashioned tastes – ever noticed those trousers he wears? Five. He goes to the top of the list. Beats Aimée hollow: she's only got three – poshness, shunning the light, and her nifty little quick-change cat stunt.

Serena's attitude was already more committed: when she spoke there was no trace of Christopher's flippancy in her voice at all. Actually, she said, very sober and precise, the list makes no mention of spooky, and Roland mostly wears jeans, so I think we can only count three. Which means he and Aimée tie.

Honestly, girl, where's your dress sense? *I* wear jeans; Roland wears joined-up mailbags that just happen to be made of denim. You know how long it took me to get mine this way? Twenty-four bleeding hours. I lay in the bath for twenty-four bleeding hours . . .

Yes, yes, we know all about your heroic past. Belt up and go on to the next. And don't say bleeding, either, it's a bit tactless in the context. The Marquise, Roland's mother, what about her?

Draccie's mum? I don't know. It's up to Viola really – she's the witness, not me. She's the only one who saw. What did the woman do, exactly, Viola? Try to be accurate: a lot hinges on this. Did she lick the stuff off her goggles? Did she slurp? How can you be so sure, then? OK, OK, an expression like that counts as a point, I reckon – *in* the context. Let's call it four, and put her down on the blacklist too. Ready for the hawthorn.

And the Marquis? Serena asked diligently.

I was all for condemnation here as well but Christopher invoked a suspended verdict. We've got to be fair, he said. The Marquis is a louche old lecher, granted, but that's no proof he's a vampire. Give him a chance first, I say, before we stake him. Give him a test.

The mere thought of testing the Marquis, let alone staking him, made me shudder. *You* give him a test, if you're so keen. For me, there's no need. He's one of them too. I think it runs in the family.

Serena nodded quickly in assent; she too looked appalled.

Christopher just laughed. Gutless swabs, the pair of you. But you'll have to do some of the fieldwork, you know, I shall be far too busy. *My* unenviable task, if you remember, is to investigate Aimée's pussy. What does the naughty thing get up to at night? What are those specks of dust among its fur? Million-dollar question: Does Aimée henna her pussy as well as her hair?

It was a game. Yes, of course it was a game. For all of us – at that stage. A pastime, a device for hijacking the attention and holding it captive for as long as possible. Christopher and Serena were bored to tears and I was distraught to tears: for our different reasons we all needed the diversion. A psychoanalyst would say I needed a scapegoat too: an embodiment-of-evil figure on to which to project my rage and misery and impotence at Sabine's plight, and thereby soothe my battered ego. After all, you can't exactly be jealous of a vampire, can you, or not in the same way a lover is jealous? (Can't you just!) Whatever it is that binds aggressor to victim, and vice versa, it's hardly a love relationship. Rivalry, jilting, dumping, betrayal – these terms no longer hold the same meaning. Your nose is broken, maybe, smashed even to pulp, but no skin off it, no lover's skin off it at all.

An analyst would also say – it's part of the creed, no? – that now I'd got my bogeyman I could be expected to calm down a bit. But that would be shrink-talk. How could I calm down, suspecting (or imagining, or hallucinating, let the shrink choose the verb) what I suspected now? Admittedly the vampire theory took care of the jealousy problem, but it rocketed the worry on Sabine's account sky-high. How could I go on doing everything in my power to nurse her back to health during the week, and then, punctually, every weekend, deliver her into the hands of a lethal predator while Ghislaine bustled tactfully off, humming snatches of Mendelssohn's wedding march, and I buckled silently down to housework? Impossible, surely, especially the 'silently' part? But equally impossible to speak, warn, utter the ludicrous, outlandish, grotesque-under-the-circumstances truth.

So what did I do, then? Well, I could give a long, tortuous answer to that question, reflecting the many tortuous things I did and thought and tried to do and tried to think, but in four short words, which are just as eloquent, I did my nut. I made a fool of myself, an unhelpful, boorish fool. In so far as I could manage, which was never far enough, I mounted guard over Sabine: sitting there at her bedside during Roland's visits, stolid and unreceptive; refusing to pick up any of Ghislaine's hints that I should leave the couple alone. I was unheeding to the point of obduracy, to the point of rudeness – who cared about manners when I stood to lose so much?

Viola, *ma petite*, could you spare a moment to help me with the vegetables? With the shopping? I have a light bulb to replace, could you come and hold the ladder for me while I . . .

A shrug, a sullen look, which it pained me to give her, and I would go on sitting. Roland will help, I would say. He's stronger. Ask Roland.

I would stare at him hard, my enemy, during these moments, aware as I did so of various under-currents of tension in the room, but principally the one strung, taut as a tripwire, between him and me. *Was* he stronger than I? He didn't look it, not just now. He looked edgy, docile, brought to heel by his need. To Ghislaine that dog-out-courting look spelt wedding bells; I just heard alarm bells. Batteries running low, eh, little bloodsucker, little junkie? How long can you hold out without a fix? That's right, smile and jump to your feet and run along to do as you are bid. No point in hurrying, I'll still be here when you get back. We'll see who can win at the waiting game.

Oh, how I hated him. And I hated myself for hating him on account of this crazy, untellable reason which seemed only to bring us closer. I knew and he knew, and that made two of us; and if he *knew* that I knew – as I sometimes felt he did – then that meant that the two of us were linked. Bound together as fast as convicts on a chain gang.

I dreamed of him, often. Complicated, shameful dreams that, on waking, made my head feel like a fusty old cinema hall: full of smoke and darkness and a flickering screen showing the tail shots of what you could tell had been a cheap, bad, sleazy movie. I was careful never to remember the film. The real-life Roland was quite enough to cope with, I could do without the subconscious versions.

Once he even asked me out on a date, if you can imagine it. Right there in the bedroom, in front of Sabine, while she was asleep. Come to Tours with me this evening, Viola. There's a good film on – Renoir, *ça pourrait te plaire*. He spoke so low that I could plausibly pretend I hadn't heard him – which is what I did. But I regretted my cowardice immediately because the mere saying of the words did something, added another tiny ply to the thread that linked us, while at the same time severing one in my link to Sabine. If I hadn't heard, then why did I look so uncomfortable all of a sudden? Why those flushed cheeks and fugitive eyes? Oh yes, they *were* flushed, *ma gamine*, oh yes, they were. And if I *had* heard, why did I not protest on Sabine's account? She would have protested sure enough had she been in my position. *Salaud*, she would have said. Dirty two-timer, you can stuff your Renoir you know where. But Sabine was different, wasn't she? And we were different, weren't we, he and I? Weren't we?

How did I bear it all without cracking? The nursing, the guarding, the hoping, the fearing, the wild muddle in my head, the stress during the daytime and the added stress of the dream-filled nights? Well, there's a short answer to this one too: I didn't. I cracked, eventually I cracked and told everything – first to Serena, who knew it already of course but only in its spoof version, not as the terrifying truth; and then, in desperation, when Serena failed me, to Sabine herself. Every dotty thing, and may I be forgiven. But that was later on, when the dotty things had become so many and so out of hand that there was no more containing them. For the moment I was trapped, swinging between the horns of my dilemma, at liberty to impale myself on the one or on the other as the momentum took me. If I decided to consider the vampire theory as real, I could be sick with fear; if I decided to view it as just a silly game of my own devising, then I could be sick with jealousy instead.

Not a happy predicament but better than Sabine's: she had no choice at all, she was sick with illness and growing daily – nightly – sicker.

XIII

The Puzzle

Sometimes I think that if he hadn't loved her – if Roland hadn't loved Sabine just that token rennet amount that starts the curdle – I wouldn't have suffered so much. His hold over her, no matter what its nature, would have been easier to endure. And the outcome too. I did, as a matter of fact, speak to an analyst once about these things, many years ago now, when Sabine's voice in my head was still sharp enough to spur me, and he told me one memorable thing: Love is never a problem, he said. Where there is love there is never a problem.

What kind of love could the man possibly have been talking about? And in what world could he have done his training?

I said at the beginning of this story that I had never until now lifted the curtain that guarded certain chambers of my mind, and that is true, I never did. But once the curtain was brusquely torn aside for me by circumstance.

I was in New York, and a friend took me to a picture gallery there. We sauntered in a little aimlessly, the way you do in galleries where there are a lot of pictures on show but none you want to see in particular – and there it was. There he was: the man in the puzzle. Unchanged. Mocking, pitying, reading right into me the way he did then, the sleeves of his dark velvet suit crimped into the same folds, his lace-ruffled hand drumming lightly on his knee in the same world-weary fashion (no, not quite the same: he was more world-weary now; we both were), while behind him the plum-coloured swathe of silk hung in its old position as it had hung for centuries, defying the laws of gravity and aesthetics in one absurd, shimmering, knotted swoop.

We meet again, Viola, he seemed to say. Last time we met was . . . let me think . . . Ah, yes, I remember now. It was in France, no? By the bedside of a sick girl? A girl you were very fond of, unless I am mistaken? That's right, it's coming back to me. You were holding one of my eyes in your hand, printed on a small piece of cardboard, and were looking for the right place in my face in which to insert it. Yes, yes, and you were smiling a triumphant little smile because you were sure, in that welter of pieces on the tray – there must have been thousands of them. Three thousand five hundred? What a good memory you have for numbers – you were sure that you had found the right piece at last. And you were smiling also because of the girl, because you thought she needed smiles around her, and there were so few occasions for wearing smiles that you wanted to make the most of this one – extract all the warmth that you could from it, maybe even get her to smile back.

And then what happened? Tell me. The smile disappeared again very quickly, of that I am sure. But why? Was it something to do with the girl again? I have a feeling that it was. I have a feeling she stretched out her hand and snatched my eye from you on its little jagged piece of cardboard and threw it back on to the tray, confounding it with the other pieces. And I have a feeling she said as she did so, in a low, gruff bleat of a voice, 'Let Roland do that bit. He wanted to do that bit. And the collar, leave that for him too. Do some background, if you must, do some sky.'

Not a very weighty exchange this, regarding a little bit of cardboard and its placing. But I had the impression, Viola, that it was weighty for you; that it caused you a great deal of pain. Correct? I thought as much. My painted eyes see a lot, you know, even in a cheap reproduction, even upside down on a tray. Ah well, that was years ago now. And how, if it's not indiscreet to ask, did it all turn out? Between the two of you, I mean? Or should I say, the three of you? Who won her in the end, that beautiful sick girl with the mane of golden hair? You, or the . . . the . . . the . . . What shall I call him? The . . .

Exactly: the what? What was he, this Roland? What were they – he, his mother, Aimée, to name the threesome we had so far focused in our sights?

Were they really (if you could use the word 'really' in this sentence and keep a straight face) vampires? If so, were they the only ones or were there more of them? The sisters, for example, the Mesdemoiselles de Vibrey – were they vampires too? And the Marquis, where did he stand? And what about the other hunt members? What about Mme Goujon, for that matter, with her lashings of beetroot soup? Perhaps it wasn't beetroot at all? It was red enough, and sticky enough, and salty enough to the taste, perhaps it was . . .

Yes, the game continued, but the more we played it, Serena and I, and the harder and better we played, the less of a game it became. Until that ghastly evening when we made the big discovery. When – for me, at least – it stopped being a game altogether, and Serena stopped being a sister, and . . .

But my memories are roller-coasting again, I must chart things one at a time, as they happened; sum up our findings in the order in which we made them. 'We' meaning just me and Serena, because Christopher's contribution to the sleuthing process was pretty well zero. Bored or not, embarrassed or not, it is just possible he might have helped a bit in the one task we had allotted him – for the sake of a few more pussy-quips, if nothing else; but that same evening of the list-making the cat disappeared from the château, never to be seen again, or not during our stay there.

This in itself I found significant, though the others didn't. I found Aimée's lack of worry on the animal's account significant too – Such a clever *minette*, it will take care of itself – when up till then she had fussed over its comings and goings during her absence considerably. Let it in, if I am not back; let it out; make sure Mme Goujon has given it its food.

Yes, always instructions in absentia: hard though we tried that evening, none of us could remember ever seeing the two of them together, cat and Aimée. None of us had ever seen her stroke it, or seen it rub itself against her legs the way it did against ours, or seen them, pet and owner, make space/time contact at all. (The evening of Matty and the *militaire*? Christopher suggested. No, not even then. First there had been the cat peering in the window and licking its paws, then there had been Aimée, licking her lips. No overlapping ever.) I hated this idea for what it implied about the past: Sabine and I in our most private, cherished moments, lying there with an ancient *voyeuse* stuck between us in cat costume, listening to our every word. But once you accepted the crazy premise, the crazy conclusions followed; logic reigns even on the far side of the looking glass.

And in true Lewis Carroll style – all that was missing was a walrus and a couple of flamingos – now came the business of the cards. At lunchtime the following day, by way of our first test, Serena pretended to trip on one of the many loose strands of the Aubusson carpet, spilling as she did so the entire contents of a box of cards right into Aimée's path. They were old cards, knockabout cards, three whole packs of them, kept constantly in a muddle. If you wanted to play a proper game with them that wasn't racing demon you always had to separate them first. What would a normal person have done in Aimée's position? Well, lunch was practically on the table; I think a normal person would have told Serena to pick the cards up, maybe, for tidyness' sake, and sort them later. Or perhaps not even sort them, just put them back in the box. But what did Aimée do? Believe it or not, she waved Serena aside with a *Maladroite*, flicking her fingers at her in that funny conjuror's way she had, and then went down on her knees and gathered the flipping things together herself and counted them. Fifty-two times three, plus the six jokers.

Christopher, still in his exuberant phase, bent down to help, making miaow noises right into Aimée's ear, and then looking up at us two and spluttering. Serena had to cross her legs: in moments of dire amusement her bladder tended to play tricks.

I don't know what there is to laugh about, Aimée chided us in her usual mild, bemused fashion as, her card-counting accomplished, we moved into the dining room and sat down to table. (Our mirth was of the long-haul, contagious variety, and Christopher was now making things worse by asking Mme Goujon if she could please bring us some garlic for the salad.) I know they are nothing special, those cards, but they serve their purpose, no? And an incomplete pack is a useless pack. Or not? Why do you want garlic, Christopher? Young people of your age should never eat garlic, it taints the breath, it is *si peu romantique*.

Oh my God. The counting and now the garlic. Aimée was right, there was nothing to laugh about, but we laughed ourselves purple all the same. While she sat there and watched us with that sweet, scatty smile, for which, on the other hand, there was justification galore. The young enjoying themselves – such a pretty sight. Let them laugh while they can. Gambol, little bunnies, gambol in the sunshine – pay no heed to the gathering storm clouds, the far-off baying of the wolves. Forewarned is not fore-armed, it is foreshadowed. And plenty of time for shadows later. How graceful he is, that dear Christopher, when he hugs his knees like that and throws back his head in profile; I can't think how he does it without falling off his chair. He ought not play around with the cutlery, of course, it is very bad manners in France to cross a knife and fork on the table, but this is not the moment to reprimand him. And Viola, such a joy to see her relaxing for a minute and forgetting that sad affair of *la pauvre* Sabine. Yes, laugh on, *petits lapins*, play on, laugh on . . .

We did too. For a while. Imagine how it was for me: rocketing, plummeting, whizzing up and down like a yoyo, now high on mirth, now low on anguish. I defy anyone to keep a sane mind in the circumstances.

Christopher came with me to see Sabine the next day, a Friday, and sat by the side of the bed opposite Roland, goggling and giggling at him the way he did at Aimée, only more blatantly, mickey-taking for all he was worth, and on that occasion I was high and low together, which almost split me. Perhaps it did. I can remember looking at their three different-coloured heads of hair – the bright champagne of Christopher's, the corvine blot of Roland's, and finally the bronze tumble of Sabine's – a little matted and pillow-worn by now – and feeling the different-coloured emotions they aroused in me, which went from dizzy mirth to dull despair, and not knowing whether to laugh or scream or cry.

I did mostly the first that day. We were a strangely merry quartet. Or merry trio, which was even better. Sabine rallied in Christopher's and my company, as if the joint presence of body-guard and jester gave her strength. She sat up, ate a huge chocolate sandwich – half a baguette with half a bar inside – then asked Christopher to do his imitation of M. Bosse and laughed so hard she had to lie down again. I had heard this piece too often to find it funny any more on its own account, but just seeing Sabine in this mood made my spirits soar. Roland laughed too, and my spirits soared even higher: it was a toady laugh, done to placate us, done to fit in with the group and Sabine knew it.

When she got up to go to the bathroom she stretched her hand out instinctively for mine, ignoring his altogether. Then, in what seemed to me a deliberate gesture of defiance, she half-trailed, half-swept her dressing gown over the puzzle tray, and when a whole wedge of completed puzzle came away, having caught on the wool of her sleeve, she shook it off carelessly so that it fell to the floor, scattering into single pieces; then she pushed at them – almost viciously – with her toes.

Never mind, said Roland in a carefully unruffled tone, stooping to retrieve those pieces that had slid under the bed, We can amuse ourselves, like Penelope, putting it together again. *On peut s'amuser*.

You can, she fired back at him. Well, not fired, but at least there was a trace of the old bark coming back into her voice. You can, Penelope. *We* would rather do something else.

We. Yes, we – beautiful, sumptuous royal plural. In fact Sabine was so tired when she returned to bed that we ended up doing nothing, but even with her dozing we were three against one that afternoon, and the one was increasingly subdued and out of countenance. He left earlier than usual, putting up no show of resistance: a kiss on the hand for Sabine, who wiped it off afterwards on the sheet, another for Ghislaine, and he was gone. A cur slinking off into the dusk. As Christopher and I bicycled back to the château along the darkening road, emptier of traffic at this time of evening, I can remember feeling almost peaceful inside for once. Sabine was better, and when she was better she was more herself, and when she was more herself she was more mine, and therefore I was better too. Not so jealous, not so mad. The anaemia, the injection marks, the game, the cards, the missing cat – all these things seemed to fit back tidily inside my head in the compartments they had always occupied, prior to my letting them loose. Crumpled puppets, stashed back into their box after the show.

He counted those frigging pieces of puzzle he picked up, Viola. Did you notice? Under his breath he was counting. That makes two of them – we've nailed two of them already. *Les deux vampires, de pire en pire.*

This Christopher sang to the strains of *Carmen*: '*L'amour est un oiseau rebelle . . .*', that bit. I joined him and we shouted the words into the rim of the forest as we sped past, and the forest sucked them up like blotting paper.

XIV

Breaking Up

In theory the coffins were our next task. Where did our vampire suspects keep their coffins with all that special home-dug earth inside? Count Dracula was run to ground – quite literally – by his pursuers when they noticed the unusually large shipments of Transylvanian soil that preceded his transfer to London. Where did Aimée keep the coffin in which she potted herself out during vegetative phases? Where did Roland and the Marquise keep theirs?

Well, just you try scuffling around the vaults of Château de Vibrey, uninvited, in the wee small hours, looking for empty coffins. Or in the daytime for that matter, looking for full ones. No, Christopher was already losing interest and had refused to accompany us, and on our own Serena and I just didn't have the guts. The long bike ride down the arterial road was daunting enough, with the *camions* lumbering past practically grazing your legs, to say nothing of gaining access to the castle without being seen or carrying out the search itself.

But what else could we do that would give us

definite proof? Because proof was what I craved now. Proof, certainty, anything to put an end to this dreadful pendulum swing between the twin instruments of torture – fear to jealousy, rack to wheel, take your pick and start all over. Sabine was better, ever since eating the chocolate sandwich she had continued to improve steadily, but how long would the improvement last? And would it last? Dr la Forge was hopeful, Ghislaine said; he was sure now it was chlorosis, and the course of chlorosis was nearly always benign.

Thus spoke la Forge M.D., for Medical Delinquent, and D.O.P., for Dirty Old Prober, into the bargain. What if he was one of them too? Wrong complexion, all that pink, but, to borrow an expression that Sabine often used when describing him as a diagnostician, I didn't trust him any further than my Flugge drops.

Time was entering into the arena as well. Had already entered, sneaky, on tiptoe, the way time does. In a mere seventeen days the summer term would be ending, and with it my attendance at this particular . . . What can I call it? School? Place of learning? Yes, place of learning will do. I wasn't sure exactly what, if anything, my father had lined up for me over the summer, but whatever it was, I was confident that with a bit of cunning and a bit of wheedling I could get him to consent to my remaining in France. To perfect my French, *bien sûr, Papa*. Maybe I could stay with Ghislaine again – that would be the ideal solution all round. Maybe she would take me as a paying guest or an au pair or something. Myself, I would go as a slave – hers and Sabine's. As slave and bodyguard, slave and blood-guard, camped in a willow cabin at their gate. What I would not, and could not, do was to abandon Sabine to the . . .

Full circle again. What *was* he, this Roland? What *were* they? Having shelved the idea of the coffin search, at least for the time being, Serena and I turned our attention to a much blander but, as it turned out, more elusive type of quarry: shadows and reflections.

The furniture of Plato's cave. Ever tried hunting for shadows and mirror images? Ever tried hunting for *missing* shadows and *missing* mirror images? In a fusty, dusty environment, what is more, where the blinds are always half-drawn and the mirrors are of a date with Versailles. The shadow world is all around us, its contents spread out flat for our inspection like bolts of material on a draper's counter – you would think it would be a cinch to spot an anomaly, but . . .

Just turn on that reading-lamp, Serena, the bright one. Train it this way and get Aimée to come here a minute on some pretext or other. Call her, tell her you've found a cockroach in the carpet. A flea, anything. Work it so that she stands right there in the pool of light, and I'll check what happens on the shadow front.

What happens is impossible to tell. Aimée runs in screaming, *Puce? Puce?* and hugs Serena to her as if for protection against a man-eating tiger. *Quelle horreur!* Where, Serena? Where? *Puces* in my house! *Jamais des puces* in my house! Oh, I detest the *puces*, horrible, *sales* little *bêtes*! Madame Goujon, come here quickly, do you see any *puces*? And Mme Goujon scurries in too, carpet beater in hand, and begins flailing the spot on the carpet indicated by Serena, and Aimée stands over her, still hugging Serena close, and the dust flies and the shadows whirl, and I am none the wiser. Except that I know now, *if* Aimée is a vampire, that vampires have a particular abhorrence for fleas, at least judging by the reaction of this one. Perhaps they see them as competition.

So it will have to be the coffins after all. We've tried virtually all the other tests, none of them conclusive. I have even taken to wearing a cross round my neck, bought cheaply in the costume-jewellery department of the Prisunic, and twiddling it in the faces of all those I encounter. To no apparent effect, except perhaps a little pained blink from Aimée's watery, early morning eyes – again, it is hard to tell. But without Christopher's zaniness the game is palling on Serena and on me too. Besides, Sabine is perkier; she needs me, she wants me by her. I have more important things to do than go grubbing around in other people's basements. Roland has exams in Paris and is absent for their duration. May he fail the lot.

* * *

145

You are going to get well, you know.

You think so, Viola? *Cent pour cent?*

I know so. *Cent pour cent.* The green's gone already – look. What shall we do when you are well enough to go out?

Nothing. Everything. *Rien de spécial* because everything is special, I never realised. Food, Viola, food is special, you have no idea. Sitting up and reading is special, with clean sheets, and the sunlight shining on your bed. Special is walking to the bathroom on your own without your head spinning or having to lean on someone else. Special is thinking about one day soon actually wanting a cigarette. I might come to England and stay with you, what about that? Would your father like me? Would he approve of me?

I approve of you, that's all that matters.

So he wouldn't, eh?

We shall see, it'll be fun to see. What do you want for supper? There's chicken, I think, if you feel like it. I'll tell Ghislaine on my way out.

Chicken. Paradise. See you tomorrow. Come as early as you can.

A week goes by, therefore, a relatively routine and tranquil week in comparison to the ones on either side, before Serena and I take advantage of an empty Thursday evening and, armed with torch and bluff courage, prise open the heavy wooden door that leads to the nether regions of the château

146

and pad our way down the stone staircase on the last stage of our quest.

Last because, yes, the game has really lost most of its charm for us now. Only the unforeseen opportunity, and a certain unwillingness to let Christopher know how important he was to the game's functioning, keep us going in this particular case. Aimée has gone to Tours to have the car serviced and has rung to say she will be back late. M. Bosse is off duty and has forgotten to give us homework. (We are cunning about inducing him to forget: all you have to do is mention Napoleon round about the close of lesson-time and he is away, gabbling on about industry and genius and the inevitable concurrence of small feet and large brains – his own feet being tiny. Dick too, according to Matty, our departed connoisseur.) Mme Goujon has a free afternoon also. From turrets to cellar, the house is ours entirely.

Down we go, then, into what our imagination has forecast will be a network of dungeons, but is in fact just one large whitewashed storeroom, brightly lit by an overhead light bulb – so the torch is superfluous – and lined on all four sides by surprisingly clean and well-arranged shelves. Most of these contain food supplies – boxes of apples, crates of potatoes, jars of bottled beetroot, bottled carrots, bottled onions, jams and other preserves – and on all of the stores, whether bottled or not, the figurative fingerprints of Mme Goujon are legible: this is clearly an outpost of her realm. It doesn't look as if Aimée has ever set foot there, let alone laid herself prostrate. In a bed of earth, what is more. Why, the place is spotless: Mme Goujon would have a fit if she came across so much as a teaspoonful of soil; even the potatoes look like they've been scraped. One wall, just a fraction more dusty than the others, is given over to wines, each bottle snugly fitted into a little round wooden hole with just its neck protruding, and in the furthest corner from where we stand, opposite the stairs, there is a pile of suitcases, half-covered by a piece of velvet curtain material. These cases, together with a pair of rusty ice skates hanging on the wall by their laces, are the only objects in the room that harbour a certain air of age and neglect: everything else could have been placed there yesterday for a glossy magazine article on good housekeeping. *Chapeau, Madame Goujon!* No wonder Aimée is such a fawning employer.

Serena and I look around, then at each another, and shrug. Relief or disappointment? Neither, simply boredom settling upon us again.

I suppose we couldn't grab a pot of those chestnuts, could we, before we go? Serena suggests. They look yummy.

I shake my head. It's all so tidy, anything added or missing would be bound to be noticed.

What about those cases?

The cases look old but ordinary, not even any interesting labels stuck on them.

What about them?

What about opening them, I mean? What about having a quick look at what's inside?

We exchange glances again, and again shrug in unison.

Probably nothing.

Yeah, you're right, probably nothing. Still . . .

Still . . .

Seeing as we're here . . .

Seeing as we're here . . .

You can bet Bluebeard's wife said just the same. I can even hear her saying it. Nothing in that little room, surely, nothing interesting at all; that's why my dear kind husband told me not to enter – in order to save me the bother. Still . . . Seeing as I'm here and have this little key . . .

The cases weren't even locked. Careless Aimée, fluffy-headed Aimée, flouting all the strictures.

Not that there was anything particularly eye-catching in any of them, or not on first inspection. A few more fancy-dress clothes, slightly more carefully kept, maybe, than the ones she had provided for the party. An oyster satin ball gown, reeking of mothballs, all baggy at the waist – perfectly hideous. An ostrich feather fan with the struts broken. A little ivory *carnet de bal*, complete with pencil. Unused, or at any rate unmarked, no names in it at all. A fox-fur cape with a crossover clasp of two little foxy faces. A sad object, but then all of these objects were sad, even the tissue paper that enveloped them had a mournful look about it, even the sheets of news-paper lining the bottom of the case.

No, not lining the bottom of the case, seeing as they were held together with a clip and had obviously been put there on purpose, *lying at* the bottom of the case. Lying at the bottom of the case and telling the truth at the bottom of the case – the stark, impossible, inescapable and horrendous truth.

I wish I hadn't learnt all that blasted French, I wish I hadn't been able to read those headings so quickly. I wish my eyes had flicked over them uncomprehending: old newspaper cuttings from God knows when. Stuff them back into the case with the rest of the clutter and forget about them. And I wish my eye and memory for clothes weren't so keen.

Because it was the dress that caught my attention. Not so much Aimée herself, who, with a freshness of face and wealth of hair I was unaccustomed to, might well have slipped my notice, particularly since most of the photographs showed her buttoned up to the nines and shrouded in a heavy motoring veil at the wheel of a far earlier model of Peugeot. Not so much the headings either, although the words *Mort*, *Tragique*, *Accident* and *Fatalité* did, it is true, have a certain arresting power of their own. Certainly not the photograph of the other victim of the crash, the younger one, Lady Beatrice Whoever-she-was, whose face and name meant nothing to me. No, it was the dress, and more exactly the neckline of the dress, that did it. A scalloped neckline, but in reverse, so that it was the skin of the wearer, not the dress, that took on the shell-shape. I remembered that dress all too clearly, it was one of the limp dressing-up togs Aimée had furnished us with on the night of the fancy-dress party. Keeping the cuttings, and keeping the clothes that feature *in* the cuttings, and keeping your name (almost intact, just a feeble consonant shift in the first letter of the surname), and keeping your habits and profession and place of residence – how slack can you get?

It can't be her. Serena was adamant. The dates don't fit. If it was her, she'd be . . . Wait, these articles don't give the woman's age, typical French, but here it says she was a *Directrice d'Académie*. Now, if she was already a *Directrice d'Académie* when she died, then that would make her, say, thirty at the least. Thirty then, so now she ought to be . . .

Mysteriously, the calculating part of my brain was still working. Just over ninety, said my voice. So that was still working too – two small bits of me running on oblivious, like the legs of a decapitated chicken.

Exactly. And she's not. Nowhere near. It must be an aunt or someone, that's all. Some relative who looked like her, and who ran the school before she did. Stop shivering like that, Viola, you're making me nervous. Let's put all this silly stuff away, back where we found it, and get out of this dump before someone comes and finds us meddling. Viola? Viola? Viola, stop it, stop doing that, you're scaring me. You don't honest to God think, do you, that . . . ? Shit! You *do*. Shit and double shit! Viola, please, say you're joking, say it's a joke. Viola! Viola! Leave off the fake hysterics, will you, it's not funny any more.

XV

Garlic and Onions

No, Serena was right, it was not funny any more. If it ever had been. In the last two deranged days we spent together before she too, like Matty and Tessa, was spirited away by anxious parents (it was lucky the telephone didn't melt under the barrage of her incandescent SOS's home), there was virtually no common ground between us at all, but on this one point we saw eye to eye: it was not funny any more.

I knew now. I knew the truth. Philosophers down the centuries have always made such a fuss about knowledge and how we come by it, but they got their priorities wrong. Acquisition of knowledge is not the problem, it's how *not* to acquire it when it's staring you in the face. Jeering at you. Thumbing its nose at you. Making a nonsense of every other bit of knowledge you have ever come by.

I was surrounded by a group of vampires. It was the modern era, the second half of the twentieth century, post-Darwin, post-Freud, post-Einstein (just), and I was stuck, helpless, hopeless, almost totally alone, in a blooming nest of vampires.

It was not my own predicament, however, that most concerned me, or I would have packed up my stuff and run there and then. Or just run – forget the packing. No, it was Sabine's. If you can count as polite the Marquise's words to me during the hunt, few and chilly though they were, all I had received from the vampire contingent so far was civility (from her), fondness (from Aimée), and a murmured invitation to the cinema. Hardly indicative of life-threatening designs on my person. With Sabine, though, it was a different matter. For some reason – maybe her greater appeal, maybe her odd-girl-outness, or maybe simply because, being older and unsupervised, she made a more available target – Sabine was on their list of victims. High on their list of victims. Heading, or so it would seem, their list of victims.

My fears had been grounded. In absurdity, OK, but grounded. Sabine had said jokingly that she wanted to be immersed in a bowl of water, like a bicycle tyre, to see where the blood was leaking from. Well, I could tell her now exactly where it was – no bowl or water required: the blood loss came from those two holes on her neck. Pints and pints of it were going out that way, leaving no trace except in the sated smile of Roland. Roland, the biped leech. The tick, the parasite, the vermin. If you were to look closely you could probably see some of it still coating his tongue when he took leave of her. If you were to kiss him soon enough afterwards – oh, banish that terrible, terrible thought – you could probably taste it.

Serena and Christopher were convinced I'd gone mad – properly, this time. They weren't far wrong. From the next morning onwards they avoided me like a leper, and in this too they were right. In my frenzy and despair I stank to heaven, the way Job did in his grief.

I had no plan, no compass, no support. I was lost in a hostile, crumbling world. I spent that night – the night of the discovery – mostly arguing with Serena in a last-ditch attempt to win her over to my side. Pleading with her, beseeching her in a kind of desperate diminuendo, first for help on all fronts, then just in the matter of guarding Sabine, and finally, when that too was denied me, holding out for a minimal, negative quota in the name of our past companionship: no hindrance, no betrayal – either to Aimée or to her parents or anyone else. This concession I finally wrung from her at about three in the morning.

I'll have no time, anyway, she flung at me as, exhausted and exasperated, we eyed one another like strangers over the crater of an overflowing ashtray before going our separate ways to bed. I'm getting out of this madhouse double quick. I'm ringing home tomorrow and then I'm off. If you've got any sense you'll do the same. Just get the hell out and try and forget this place exists; then you might be OK.

What do you think I should do about Christopher? I asked. (Apart from 'Goodbye' I think these were practically the last words I ever spoke to her. It's hard to speak to someone who won't remain in the same room with you: already at this stage she had gained the doorway.)

What do you mean, *do* about him?

Do you think I should get him to promise secrecy too?

Oh, leave Christopher, she said in a throwaway voice that came to me through the gap of the rapidly closing door. He's not going to grass, he doesn't give a shit.

Lucky Christopher. But then, not so lucky either, just that much more cocooned in his detachment. During dinner – which for me had been an ordeal: speaking levelly to Aimée when I knew she had been dead for the past sixty years, smiling at her, spooning down my food without retching, and letting none of my horror show – he had just sat with his head thrown back and rolled bread pellets. Hysterical girl stuff; nothing to do with him. (Oh, but it was, my old school friend. Tell me, how do you behave at mealtimes now?)

I slept like a log that night – what remained of it. I was young, and the young sleep, no matter what. In the morning I awoke with total awareness of the way things stood, which was unusual for me and probably meant that I had slept like a log travelling through whirlpools. My head, primed with information though it was, was still totally empty of plans: the knowledge was there, the fears were there, but they just rattled around inside my skull – dried peas in a jar, taking on no pattern whatsoever.

Almost without realising how I had got there – had I been sly about missing lessons? Had I spoken to anyone about where I was going? – I found myself at some point of the morning on a bicycle, fully dressed but hungry, pedalling hectically along the road in the direction of Sabine's. Some kind of pea-formation must have clustered and propelled me. Curled in the basket in front of me was a long plait of garlic bulbs: I wasn't sure how that had got there either; presumably I had bought it on the way.

Not long after this, judging by the sun and the hunger, which were both on a gradual rise, I was standing in the doorway of Ghislaine's kitchen, watching her as, with a skin-diver's mask over her face to protect her eyes, she sat at a deal table, chopping onions and other ingredients for a stew.

How long I stood there before entering, I don't know – I was still in this funny trance-like state that made time so difficult to measure – but it was long enough for the scene to exert a slightly calming effect on the contents of the pea-jar, and to imprint itself on my memory under the title, 'Last Glimpse of Home'. Ghislaine had a Midas touch where grace was concerned, and like Midas's it operated automatically, independent of her will. Aesthetics can't have been much on her mind that morning, and yet the table top could have served as a model for a Cézanne still life, so beautifully did the coloured pot and vegetables bask there in the sunlight, and she herself, with her long arched neck and looped-back, greying hair framing her sideways-tilted face, could have sat for a Modigliani portrait. Only the mask spoke of the artistic revolution to come.

She took it off when she saw me, and I noticed that behind it the tears were flowing just as copiously as if she hadn't been wearing it at all. For a moment my reasoning stayed trustingly with the onions. Then, as I moved closer, I saw the colour of her eyes: deep olive, almost khaki, and in a flash my mind lurched forward into the terror zone. It was Sabine. I knew it was Sabine: she was worse again. Not *much* worse, or Ghislaine wouldn't have been in the kitchen at all, she'd have been in the sickroom, but worse. Significantly worse.

What's happened, Ghislaine? For God's sake, tell me quick. There's been a relapse, hasn't there?

She nodded, and wiped the tears angrily away with the corner of a chequered dishcloth.

It's so stupid of me, forgive me, *ma petite*, but I can't help it. It's nothing serious, I'm sure, just a temporary setback. A fluctuation, like Dr la Forge says, in the normal course of the disease. Nothing to worry about. And I don't worry, she went on quickly, flashing me a wild, unconvincing smile,

I'm not worrying. It's just that . . . Things were going so well, and now . . .

Roland is back, isn't he.

It wasn't a question, I didn't ask it, I just said it.

Her face lit up with a proper smile now, although only a thin, wistful one, and she took my hand and brushed it against her cheek: a soothing measure to counteract my jealousy.

Oh, yes, thank goodness, he is back. He came last night, just before it happened. I would have preferred you, of course, my little English nurse who needs no instructions, but, *tu vois*, it was such a comfort to have someone with me.

Tu vois, tu sais, tu comprends. Yes, I saw all right, and I knew and I understood – what had happened, what was happening and what was going to happen – but still I was powerless. And still without anything I could call a plan. Knowledge, a cheap cross and a plait of garlic – these were all I had at my disposal. The temptation to throw myself into Ghislaine's arms and blurt out everything was so strong that I had to hold on to the edge of the table to stop myself. Clutch at it hard and bite the inside of my cheeks, too, until they hurt. If I faltered and unburdened myself on her kind, welcoming shoulder she would never let me near Sabine again. Motherly, yes, but she was Sabine's mother, not mine, and I must remember this. She would listen to my rantings with a sampler of expressions on her face that would go from surprise to anger, passing through disbelief, irony, dismay and stupefaction on the way, and ending up, like as not, at sheer naked fright. Poor Viola, jealousy has affected her reason. She would call up Aimée, and Aimée would flap and telephone my father, and probably plunge me into a cold bath for good measure while she waited for the call to come through. Then she would summon Dr la Forge, and he would diagnose a *crise de nerfs* – a nervous breakdown due to stress – and prescribe rest and tonic and segregation, and I would be dragged away and sedated and put to bed in a darkened room and left there helpless while Aimée and her vampire cronies . . . I could see it all, clear as if it had already happened. No, I must resist, must combat that pathetic chick instinct to run to the hen-bird for protection in time of danger. My only hope now – our only hope now – lay with Sabine herself.

Can I go up and see her?

Of course you can, Viola, she would love it. Only go quietly. Don't wake her if she's sleeping. She needs sleep, this morning she looked so tired that I . . . Oh, I'm sorry, pay no attention – these wretched onions . . .

The sickbed scene that followed was what Aimée would have called *pénible* – a word she used often, particularly in regard to the regrettable state of her most valued possessions such as the carpet, the piano, the screen, and the upholstery of the Peugeot. (That's what comes of living so long, you old mutant, and being so tight with your money. Why not splash out on the first of each century? Be a devil. Should be easy when you're half one already.) I knew it would be so – *pénible*, pathetic – but I had to play my part. I had at least to try.

Sabine was not asleep, although I would have had no qualms about waking her if she had been: I had deliberately left Ghislaine's request on this point unanswered. She was lying there motionless, propped up on the pillows in an artificial, ceremonious-looking fashion, as if arranged by some energy other than her own. Her hands stuck out stiffly like a doll's, palms to the ceiling; her hair too had a doll-like quality about it: brushed tidily at the front but not at the back. Strands of it stuck to the pillowcase at odd angles to the head: by these dull gold rays against their white backdrop I was reminded of a monstrance.

Perhaps this was one reason why I dropped down on my knees by her bedside. Another was in order to strew the garlic under the bed without her seeing. And the third was to beg her forgiveness before I started on my outlandish tale. What I had to do seemed so cruel. I already knew it would serve no purpose other than upsetting her and weakening her further. It wouldn't even make her laugh, or not for long.

Well? (*Alors?* Oh, that ductile word of hers, what was it now? So faint it was almost a sigh. How *could* he have done this to her? How *could* he, how could anyone?) Well, what is it, Viola? Can't be that bad. Go on, *vas-y*, spit it out. My schedule for today is pretty empty, you can take all morning.

I spat all right. I spewed. After a few initial stumbles, especially over the key term 'vampire', which I had to expel by force it rang so dotty, the words came spilling out of me like corn from a sack, abundant, unstoppable. And virtually impossible to stuff back into the sack again, although Sabine's first reaction, when the last grains hit the floor, was, predictably, to make me try.

What was all that? A comic turn to take my mind off things? Who do you think you are: *foutu* Fernandel?

Yes, some of her remarks, like this one, I remember verbatim, but only very few. The others, the harsh ones, the scornful, lacerating ones that cost her such effort to deliver and me such pain to hear her deliver, are fortunately lost to my memory. Only the gist remains, the gist and the bitter, bitter flavour of defeat. The blight was back; it lay like a poisonous film between us, thin but impeding contact. Her body was there for me to see, her hand was mine to clasp, to press, to prise its fingers open with my own and grip it – tight, as tight as you would grip the hand of someone drowning or hanging from a precipice. Her neck was there for me to clasp the cross around; her head was there above it for me to lay my face against and hiss in desperation in her ear, *Crois-moi, je te supplie.*

Wear this for my sake. What does it cost you? What does it cost you? Just a silly, tinny cross – but inside it she was his already.

Do I have to spell it out to you, Viola? I'm knackered, can't you see? I've had this frightful night – *épouvantable*. It's all I need now, to have to give a lecture on teenage psychology. Look into yourself – you know perfectly well what the score is: you're tired too, you're worried, you hate him and you're jealous. No, sorry, hate is wrong, and that's where the knot is. But forgive me if I leave you to unravel it on your own. I'm just too tired, see? Too darn tired. And as for the other stuff – your phobia of penetration and whatnot, because, don't kid yourself, that's all the vampire symbol stands for – if you have any pity just cut it out and help save me the oxygen.

That was more or less what she said to me. No, less, definitely, because I've omitted the swear words and some of the more scathing psycho-jargon regarding things like long incisors and rape fantasies and worse. I was jealous of Roland, jealous of her, jealous of their closeness, from which I stupidly saw myself as excluded. (Although I'd certainly *get* myself excluded if I went on like this, and pretty smartly too.) I was inhibited, I was raw and hysterical and immature and twisted, and all hung up about sex and the male. It was pathetic, the lengths I was prepared to go to in order not to face up to these few simple facts. It was unworthy of me; it was cruel and thoughtless and selfish. And it was so *foutu* boring, it made her scream. Or would do if she could find the breath. Please, Viola, please. I'd begged of *her*, now she was begging of me, would I come to my senses – now, this minute – and admit the whole thing had been a stupid tasteless joke, or else just belt up and get out and leave her in peace.

I had planted the garlic, and in her agitation Sabine seemed to have forgotten about the cross, which was still fastened round her neck. It was only the size of an acorn, hopefully she wouldn't notice and would leave it there. Hopefully he *would* notice and, what with that and the aroma of hidden garlic, be foiled, at least for tonight. What else could I do now but obey her wishes and abandon her to her fate?

Well, I could crouch outside the door in tears for one thing, but only until her voice reached me and told me not to.

I know you're still there. Do you recant, Viola? Do you take it all back?

Like Galileo?

Like Galileo, my *foutu* foot. You poor dope, you don't even know what science is.

Not bad, for the last spoken exchange between us. I doubt even Billy Wilder could have thought up a better. Shut up and deal, Viola. Nobody's perfect. You don't even know what science is.

XVI

The Rule of the Game

Not yet belief or understanding, because what I blurted out to him was just a confused torrent of words, but sympathy and support – yes, these came in the end from where I least expected: my father.

I rang him in the early afternoon when I arrived back at the château, still hungry but with no prospect of food because lunch was already over.

When I was a child he had once spotted me from afar on the roof, walking the cornice for a dare. A school friend had put me up to it – a certain Imogen Black-Spinner whose name was the only thing my father liked about her. It was about a foot and a half wide, this cornice, and I was accompanied on the enterprise by my dog. Neither of us were greatly impressed or rattled by what we were doing – we had done it in parts several times before but never the whole way round.

I remember my father's spirit-level voice, hardly a raise in it at all, hardly an inflection, despite the distance it had to travel: I'd come down now, Viola, if I were you. No, don't turn there, go on a little bit,

that's right, and turn . . . Yes, there, that's right.
And now go back, slowly, slowly – don't mind
about the dog, he's got four legs, he'll manage fine
– slowly, slowly, back to the window you got out of,
and then . . .

He was like that now: the same voice, the same
gentle precision perfectly masking the urgency that
lay beneath. In answer to my garbled request that he
come out immediately, to fetch me, help me, protect
me – I wasn't quite sure which, maybe all three; I
just couldn't hold out on my own any longer with
these terrifying creatures hemming me in on every
side – he made no objection at all.

My sweet, don't, don't. There's no need for you
to try to explain anything. Especially not over this
appalling line. Stay calm. I'm coming. I'll be with
you in – whatever it takes. At the latest by tomorrow evening. I'll drop everything. No, no, how
could it be too much trouble? You come first in
my thoughts – always. My bottle of water is never
trouble, you know that, don't you? Trouble goes
with strife, and that's another story. No, no worries
about sleeping arrangements either: we'll find a
hotel or something, we'll work it out later. Just
pass me over to Madame Whatshername a
second . . . No? All right, all right, no. Whatever
you say, my lovekin. But she's there, right? You're
there? Fine, well, just stay there, stay put and wait
until I come. Tomorrow, tomorrow. Tomorrow
that ever is, I promise.

It was like magic, like the steadying hand of our local blacksmith on the pastern of a nervy horse. I could almost hear myself blowing through my nostrils in relief as my muscles relaxed. My dad who loved me. In whose thoughts I came first. Here by my side. Tomorrow that ever was. Why, oh, why hadn't I turned to him earlier? He knew my mind better than anyone; *he* knew I wasn't mad; he would listen and he would sympathise, and in some way – leave it to him to find one – he would pluck me from this nightmare and bring me to safety.

What about Sabine, though? Could he do the same for her? Ah, that was another matter and another question. I doubted that he could, not straight off: he had no authority where Sabine was concerned. And it was unlikely that Ghislaine, who did have the authority, or a certain amount of it, would allow her to travel in her present state. However, even here, in this darkest section of the tunnel, it at last seemed to me that I could see a glimmer of light. Obscured by a fog of ifs, but light all the same.

My chain of reasoning went like this: *if* I could persuade my father to stay on here a few days (a fairly big if, once he knew the score: he was no coward, but physical courage was not his strong suit, he was even scared of moths); *if* I could persuade him to stay on, though, and *if* during that time the two of us together could successfully protect Sabine from Roland until she got her strength back, then (always depending *if* Sabine and Ghislaine were willing, and *if* Dr la Forge raised no opposition) we could whisk her away to England with us when we left. Home, to England and to safety.

A plan at last, or a shred of one. But it too hinged on yet another if – the fifth: it might work, it could conceivably work, but only *if* I could shepherd Sabine through this last lonely night acting on my own resources.

What were my chances here? Miserably slight. Two of my resources – the garlic and the cross – I had deployed already, leaving me with only my knowledge. My cruel, sterile knowledge, which, like a cancer specialist's, enabled me to predict but not prevent. What other weapons had I, a girl of seventeen, against . . . ?

Oh yes, I know, but it took courage to acknowledge it: the answer was there, implicit in the question. Explicit, in fact, and too bad if it came accompanied by icy sweat and a wave of nausea. I was a girl and I was seventeen, and he'd batted his eyelashes at me the first time he saw me, and he'd asked me out on a date already. Just one more telephone call, Viola – you said there was a thread between you, no? Well, go on, give it a yank – and then back to the mirror with you, and to the scent bottle and the make-up box and all the tricks. Or to the butcher's shop if you prefer. Mind you deck it out nicely, the meat, the bait, the decoy. Package it well: nice crisp wrappings, a sprig of rosemary, an eye-catching tag: 'Prime English Cut, Last Day, Special Offer'.

How difficult it is to tell this part of my story and how reluctant I am to tell it. Because to tell it entails drawing aside an even thicker set of curtains and reliving, in some cramped but still operative dimension, those shameful moments – in intention perhaps the only real act of heroism I have ever attempted, but in practice a queasy amalgam of brazenness and fright. My voice, which didn't even sound like mine, so coy and teasing it came across, pronouncing his name, that loathsome name I never willingly uttered; sticking it in the same sentence as my own, so close they were almost touching: Roland? Roland, this is Viola. Yes, Viola. Yes, *vraiment*. I was ringing to ask you . . . I was wondering . . . er . . . I was wondering if the cinema offer was still valid. You know . . . that time you asked me to go with you to the cinema, remember? Because if it is, then maybe this eveni— It *is*? Oh, that's . . . that's terrific. *Formidable*. Mmm. Yeah. Great. See you at seven, then. *A tout à l'heure.*

And that was only the start. What followed . . . Oh, I don't know that I can bear to plunge again into such murky waters. Can I? Must I? And what is it exactly that this shame is caused by, its wound so deep it still smarts after all these years? By the fact that I dolled myself up like a siren? No, not that. By the fact that I was in effect aiming to steal my lover's

169

lover, albeit with the best intentions? No, not that either. By the despicable, unbidden frisson that his nearness gave me – similar to the one I'd had foisted on me by Dr la Forge's forefinger and in roughly the same place? Not even, not even that. No, the cause of the shame is ignorance again – my deplorable, vulnerable ignorance. That is what riles me, that is what stings. Everyone knows, everyone knows but Viola.

Anyway, if tell I must, let me get on with it. He came to fetch me. Punctually at seven. All lanky and laid-back and smiling, leaping out of the car to meet me and giving only the faintest of starts at my appearance, as if it happened to him every evening to go out with a seventeen-year-old rookie whore. Good news, we'd struck lucky: by a fluke there was another Renoir film showing. Not the one he had wanted to see, a slightly older one, but well worth seeing none the less. *La Règle du Jeu*. Only we must hurry because it began at a quarter to eight.

Aimée smiled approvingly at this, to her, totally meaningless piece of news as she consigned me into the predator's hands. In fact she had smiled approvingly from the moment she had learned I was going out with him. (*Esprit de corps* – yes, I suppose you could call it that.) *La Règle du Jeu*, what a pretty title! Enjoy yourselves, now, the pair of you. You both deserve a little *récréation*. Drive carefully, Roland, won't you, and come back immediately the film is finished. I'll ask Madame Goujon to leave you out something to eat. I know Viola is safe with you – no one safer – but I shall sit up for her all the same.

Or perhaps stand up was what she had in mind? Usher us into the salon with sandwiches and leave us there, and then stand outside in the darkness behind the window panes and hope for another live show? Well, if so, she was in for a disappointment. Whatever I found myself obliged to do in order to keep Roland occupied and away from Sabine, I certainly wouldn't do it with Aimée looking on. Not any more. And if that cat should turn up I, who loved cats dearly, or most of them, would kick the lousy beast as far as Belgium.

And yet in the end it went a bit like that. The cinema was bearable – just: I remember nothing of the film save for the name Schumacher (pronounced the French way, Shoomashair), which still bothers me today, to the point that I never watch car racing if I can help it. I can't watch the film either, which is a pity, since they say it is one of the finest ever made.

The whole way through, you see, I was conscious only of this being beside me. This strange, alluring/repellent being who had the effrontery, while I was a jangling mass of nerves, to sprawl there at my elbow in a pose of the utmost relaxation and munch on – whatever it was he was munching. Some kind of peppermint affair: for the carnivore, breath does pose a problem. He offered me one, but like

Persephone I'd have died sooner than accept so much as a grain of nourishment from his hands. Now and again he would give a little heave in his chair and from his mouth would come a smothered chuckle. More than relaxed, he was amused. And not only, or even chiefly, by the film. I could tell that. No, he was amused by me and by the situation. I had striven to seduce, gone all out to seduce, entice, arouse, and seemingly all I aroused in him was this infuriating amusement and perhaps, perhaps – although this thought was so bewildering I could hardly fit it in my head – a feeling of tenderness. I had the distinct impression that although he knew I hated him, and probably had no illusions as to why I had telephoned him, hatred and all, he didn't hate me back in the slightest – quite the reverse.

In one of the saddest parts of the film – the close-up of a dying rabbit, I think it was – he took my hand, turned it over and brushed the inside of my wrist against his lips. I bucked like a rabbit myself, expecting to feel the pressure of his teeth and then the bite – there were veins there, too, were there not? But all that followed was the gentle relinquishment of my hand, its replacement in my lap, and then that tiny heave again as he leant towards me and tapped, as his father had done before him, a teasing finger on the tip of my nose.

Ça va, Viola? You're not bored? You can follow all right?

I couldn't follow, not a word except for Shoomas-hair, but I was not bored. I doubt Andromeda was bored either as she waited for the sea serpent. (What *would* Sabine say to that comparison, I wonder? Unprintable.) I was terrified, keyed up to breaking point, hungrier than I'd ever been in my life before but with no desire to eat, my stomach having turned itself at some point of the day into a bowl of sulphuric acid with the lid on, but bored, no, that I was not.

Nor was I bored on the drive back to the château, awaiting as I did, at any moment, a sudden swerve off the road and into one of the lanes that led into the forest and then, in silence, in the darkness, the aggression, the assault. (Only maybe it wasn't like that at all. Maybe it was more a Svengali business, a hypnotic stare, a look-into-my-eyes-and-do-not-flinch-as-I-come-closer sort of approach.) But with ruthless honesty, as kilometre after kilometre passed without mishap and the road became more and more familiar as we neared the final stretch, I had to admit to a certain feeling of letdown along with the panic.

Could it be that it was worse to be spurned by a vampire than it was to be attacked by one?

Well, yes, if the rejection spelled tactical failure too. Because how could I ensnare my predator/prey and keep him successfully away from Sabine until daybreak if he declined point blank to enter the snare? So little time if you looked at it backwards and saw it dwindling; so much if you looked at it forwards, stretching out like a via dolorosa to be trod.

Roland? (Husky, come-hither voice, well, the husky part wasn't difficult.) Do we *have* to go back so soon? Couldn't we just pull in somewhere and stop for a moment? And talk, maybe?

No answer. And the luscious profile remained fixed: he was obeying Aimée's instructions and driving like an undertaker. (At whose funeral? Whose?)

Just talk? Just a moment?

Still no answer, but in the light of the dashboard I thought I saw his mouth flex upwards at the corner. Another smile, sod him. Another fond avuncular smile.

And then, unexpectedly, his hand straying from the steering wheel for a brief moment and covering mine, giving it a quick little non-avuncular squeeze.

Viola. Oh, Viola, it's not as easy as you think. *C'est pas si simple que ça.*

We hadn't spoken of Sabine all evening. If he were to do so now, I realised, then that would be the end of it – her name would come down between us like a blade, severing this weird connecting thread, which I could *still* feel, despite everything. He was behaving impeccably – as uncle, friend, elder brother, call it what you like – but the thread was there and he was drawn by it. He was tempted.

Proof was that he made no mention of Sabine. But by now the car was drawing close to the château gates. I could pick out the spearlike rods of the railings already and through them, in flashes, the glimmer of the lantern that hung over the doorway. It was dreadful, it was humiliating, I didn't even feel relieved on my own account, merely anguish-ridden on Sabine's: it was not going to work, my seduction plan was not going to work. As a last desperate measure I resolved to wait until the car braked for the swing over the road and into the drive, and then throw myself across Roland and pull the steering wheel hard in the opposite direction, hopefully landing us up on the verge. There was no traffic and the verge was wide and flat, almost a lay-by, it shouldn't be dangerous; the dangerous bit would come after, when I would have to face the consequences of my gesture. Whatever they might be.

I don't know whether I would ever actually have had the nerve to carry out this manoeuvre. I think I would but I'm not sure: I had already shut my eyes and braced myself for action, but as things turned out I merely stayed braced and opened them again. Because, quite of his own accord, Roland suddenly slowed down the car and turned it off the road, parking it only about ten yards short of the spot I had chosen as my deadline. Then he switched off the ignition and turned to me, taking my head between his hands and holding it tight but with care, as if it were a bowlful of liquid that was threatening to spill.

I could see very little of him, it was so dark, only

the glimmer of his eyeballs; they moved sideways fast, to and fro, to and fro, so that I could tell he was shaking his head. Then he clicked his tongue, also rapidly.

Rien à faire, little Viola. Nothing doing, nothing doing.

I wanted to say something – deny, protest, voice surprise, indignation, something – but his hands forestalled me, swivelling, one to behind my neck and the other to the front, covering my mouth.

Ssssh, ssssh. Ttt, ttt, ttt. Listen to me, Viola. Don't get me wrong, don't take this badly, but it's no good. Understand? It's no good. Whatever's going on in this pretty head of yours – and it *is* a pretty head, it is, oh, *such* a pretty head – you must convince yourself, it's just not going to work.

I made a mooing noise through his hand which he must have interpreted as a 'why not?' and perhaps it was.

Because . . . Because . . . Because of many things. But it will never work, not the way you want it to. Not the way I want it to either maybe. Things are written differently. It's not ours to change them. *C'est clair*?

He kissed me then. Not on my lips, seeing that his hand was still sealing them, but on that cursed nose of mine again and on the eyelids. Peck, peck, peck, about as sexy and threatening as a nanny. Then he withdrew his hand and fumbled in his shirt pocket for a cigarette. He lit two and gave me one, then repeated his question, *C'est clair?*

Clear as mud, Mr Vampire. Clear as blood. What *was* going on here? What was he referring to when he said it wouldn't work? To the escapade between the two of us? Or to my plan, my defence of Sabine? How much did he know? How much did he reckon I knew? Was his a double-decker answer? If so, did he expect me to read it on both levels, or just on one, or . . . ?

Oh, this fiddly rapier nonsense, it was driving me mad – all this feinting and parrying and finesse and *double-* and *triple-entendres*. Speaking would get me nowhere, only into a deeper and deeper muddle. Better just to shelve the language of words and rely on the older, wiser one of the body.

A body conversation with a vampire, though? Would our vocabulary be the same? Necking, for example, how would necking translate into Vampirese? Or love-bites? How, even, a French kiss?

Don't think about that, you craven idiot, think of nothing but Sabine. Think of her lying there under the open window like a limp little dummy – drained of strength, defenceless, at his mercy. Think that this is all you can do now to save her, to win time, win time. Think: every second lost to him, a second gained to her. Think . . . No, better still, don't think at all; act.

So, shutting my eyes again – clamping them tight, battening down all of my sense-equipment so that I

177

neither saw nor smelt nor felt nor heard anything save this bare imperative cracking in my head like a whip – I hurled myself, as far as this was possible within the confines of the car, on to Roland's chest and clung there, murmuring some kind of sentimental gibberish, the wording of which I prefer not to recall. It has little importance, anyway, because it soon turned out that I had battened my senses down so tight and emptied my mind so thoroughly I had clean forgotten about the cigarettes.

Roland's, which he had dropped under the impact of my chest against his, landed in the space between the seat and the door, and was retrieved by him with alacrity at the first whiff of burning carpet. Which came very shortly afterwards, leaving me uncertain as to whether he thrust me aside on that account or simply in order to shake himself free. Mine was untraceable save for the continued smell of burning, which grew and grew and thickened and thickened until we were obliged to interrupt all traffic between us, in whatever direction it might have flowed and wherever it might have led us, and run to the house for water.

End of evening, end of rescue attempt; for me, virtually end of hope as well. Once the fire brigade lark was over, there was no alternative but to sit in Aimée's dining room making awkward three-way conversation under her faraway but oh so beady gaze that didn't miss a trick, not a trick.

Curieux, the way that cigarette landed up where

it did. And the car – a little *curieux* too. Why was it parked outside the gate? Why did you not drive it up to the front door, Roland? Ah, the smoke, *c'est ça*, of course, the burning – there was not time. Of course, of course.

It was not her way to show disapproval – it didn't fit with her loose-reined style – but she seemed to be at the very least disappointed in some important respect with her young vampire colleague. As he ate she eyed him balefully, pushing crossly at her tendrils of escaping hair as if to convey her displeasure through their medium. There was clearly no question now of her leaving me alone with him, or even pretending to do so. She wanted him gone, fast, and made no secret of the fact, carrying on nimbly from one hint to the next.

And speaking of time, *mes enfants*, it is twenty past eleven; the others have gone to bed already, and Viola needs a good rest – her father is due to arrive tomorrow (a little warning note rang on these two words, *son père*, as if his arrival was something to be feared. Good sign.) So, Roland, if you don't mind hurrying a little with that consommé . . .

Roland didn't mind a bit. He downed the soup in a gulp – not a pretty spectacle to watch, this rapid disposal of the russet-brown liquid – kissed Aimée's hand, said goodnight to both of us, and was gone. And that was that. Much as I yearned to, I could do nothing more. He had the car, I only a bicycle; if his bloodlust took him to Sabine he would be quenched and through before I was even halfway there. Quite apart from the fact that if he wanted to travel even quicker he could probably turn into a bat, spread his wings and fly. All I could do now was to rely on a twist of garlic and a little metal cross, and hope for . . . no question of the best but at any rate the least worst: her overnight survival.

XVII

Help

Next morning there was a feel of lawlessness in the château. Not that any rules had been strict, ever, but they had been there, been in place: a few thin strands, holding things together like twine round a bunch of asparagus. Now, school, staff, students, structure, everything seemed to flop apart.

When I woke up, Christopher already had his music on loud, Aimée was nowhere to be seen, and Serena was thumping around the place waving bits of clothing, packing in a flurry. She was due to leave for Paris by train that morning. *Bon voyage*, my half-hearted dilettante vampire-chaser; make way for the pros. Breakfast had been laid, lightly mauled by the others, and then left there to congeal in the slatted sunlight. No sign of Mme Goujon either, nor of the little beaded muslin cloths that she used for covering the butter and the jam pots.

I shooed away the wasps and downed a croissant for the sake of my body – which didn't seem to appreciate it much, as it left it lying at the entrance of my stomach like an uncollected parcel – and then mounted my bike and set off without a word to anyone.

What colour would the litmus paper of Ghislaine's eyes show this morning? This was the only question my head seemed to have room for. I dreaded learning the answer. Dreaded encountering her look, dreaded seeing what I knew I would see there: that dull clouding of despair. No coincidence that in the hasty snapshot world of cliché hope is green.

And yet I must have undervalued the powers of those two traditional, homespun remedies: holy cross and garlic. Or else I had kept Roland up late enough after all, and after leaving me he had gone straight home to bed, as disoriented as I was by the night's unfolding events. Or else the consommé had blunted his appetite. Because when I finally found myself standing face to face with Ghislaine, who was sitting quietly writing letters at her desk in the room adjoining Sabine's, I saw, with a surge of joy so strong it nearly made me dizzy, that things were better. I didn't even have to check her irises, her smile was so wide.

She's sleeping, Viola, isn't it wonderful? She's had a good night, she's eaten breakfast. It was as Dr la Forge said: just a temporary setback. Oh, the relief! I thought we were in for another attack, but now – I feel it in my bones, a mother knows these things – she's on the mend at last, really and truly. She's going to pull through.

Of course she was because if need be I was going to pull her through myself. My father and I in partnership, we were going to pull her. Sabine had weathered this last crucial night with only the flimsiest of safeguards; from now on everything would be easier. From now on we would have an adult on our side – a clever, wily, resourceful adult who would never let himself be bested by a group of resuscitated French freaks.

I said earlier that the day of the fancy-dress ball was my last unclouded day, but I was overlooking this one. This, in its precarious rim-of-the-volcano way, was a luminous day too. Sitting there chatting to Ghislaine, weaving in my head as I did so an absurd but oh so comforting fantasy of bringing her and my father together, and their falling in love and marrying, and our living, all four of us, in my father's house, which would then spring alive under Ghislaine's magic ministrations. (I had to eliminate the boys from my fantasy: not even in a dream dimension would they fit into my father's fastidious lifestyle. And I had to exclude the house-helpers too because I couldn't see them adapting very comfortably to a foreign regime. Never mind, Ghislaine and I would manage the housework, we made a good team.) Every so often I poked my head into the bedroom and watched Sabine as she lay there, bathed in the sunlight she so craved, the little cross still glinting in the hollow of her neck – my sacred place. Watched a strand of hair that fell across her face billow backwards and forwards like a golden metronome in time to her regular breathing. It was turning glossy again already, her hair, and so was she. Ghislaine's maternal radar system had sounded correctly: the menacing presence of illness could no longer be felt. Gone was yesterday's doll. The room smelt fresh if a bit garlicky; wholesome and vital. Coffee aroma in place of the tang of medicine. A whiff of toothpaste. Soon there might be cigarette smoke as well. Roll on the Gauloises in their blue packets with their victory wings.

I tiptoed in and sat on the floor for a bit beside the bed, my face, like Sabine's, turned towards the sun. I remember that, and I remember how nice it felt – those bright rays dancing on my skin. At some point I think I may have joined her briefly in sleep. Minutes wasted, minutes stupidly squandered, because sleep is not a place you join anyone, but how was I to know they were so precious?

Around midday I rang Aimée to let her know where I was, and to find out if my father had called, and if so, from where. By the slightly cramped feeling in my stomach as I waited for her answer I realised how closely my present mood of optimism was tied to his arrival. Had she said, No call yet, my hopes would have crashed again. Had she said, From the coast, they would have stayed about level. Had she said, Paris, they would have risen quite a bit. As it was, they rocketed because she said, Yes, *mais oui, mais oui, mais oui, petit lapin*, and to come back as soon as I could: he had rung from Chartres, where he was resting for a while, having crossed the Channel late yesterday evening and then driven through the night. He would be leaving the moment it was cool enough for him to set out again and should arrive sometime in the afternoon. *Les Anglais* and their horror of driving in the heat! If you asked her, in weather like this, behind the wheel was the best place to be.

Even when driving veils were the fashion, Aimée? Even when you were muffled up like a mummy and the dust flew everywhere? Even when you crashed with poor Lady Whatever-her-name-was and sent her to an early grave? I was tempted to say something like this, just to startle her, but I didn't, of course. My father had taught me virtually nothing, and permitted others to teach me very little, but one thing I did remember him telling me, probably in connection with chess, was: if your opponent under-estimates your intelligence the battle is half won.

When your intelligence is zero, though, how can an enemy underestimate it? My father's rule of thumb made no provision for that. I ate *pot au feu* with Ghislaine in the kitchen, then took a bowl up for Sabine but she was still asleep. Deeply, soundly, or so it seemed, snoring a bit but in a light, snuffly way, like a pug-dog. There was no need to worry about an afternoon visit from Roland: Ghislaine had mentioned that his mother had commandeered him for the day. The de Vibreys were holding some kind of *réception* that evening, she said with a smile (whose significance escaped me, along with so much else), and he wouldn't be round till late. Late was bearable, late was OK; my father would have arrived by that time and he would ensure that no evil befell. I planted a goodbye kiss on the top of Sabine's head and she stopped snuffling and turned over quickly – so quickly I had the impression she was aware of my presence. A fact that, stupidly, pleased me at the time. Then I went downstairs, took leave of Ghislaine, got on my bike again and trundled down the road I had trundled down so many times before, leaving a snatch of Mozart in the forest this time to add to the bayings and sighings and roarings and horn-calls and all the other noises encrypted there. '*Voi che sapete*'. My father's favourite aria. You who are in the know. Honestly, life can sometimes be so trite you'd think it had been scripted by a hack.

At four o'clock, the great arrival. Aimée, chiefly through the agency of Mme Goujon, I suspect, had somehow in the meantime got her housewifely asparagus bundled up again and fastened with a hasty cordon. The guest bedroom had been made up tidily, with books and flowers on the bedside table, and on the bed, embroidered linen sheets in only the palest shade of off-white. *Inpensable*, she warbled at me as she added the final touches, to send my father to a hotel. With Christopher's parents it was different, they were flying out together and would be staying the night at the Lion d'Or, but a man alone – *tout seul comme ça* . . .

So Christopher's mother and father were arriving too. It was the first I had heard of this. A veritable epidemic of anxiety seemed to have broken out among our parents. Well, that accounted for the sudden upswing on the housekeeping front: Aimée was aiming to placate her clientele. The salon was dust-free for a change, or almost, the gilt spots on the screen glinting brightly in the zebra-crossing strips of daylight, the Aubusson carpet exhibiting – although again, only where the tongues of light struck it – hitherto unsuspected traces of green and pink. Tea was set out in the dining room on a lavish scale by Aimée's standards: biscuits, squares of local chocolate, crystallised fruits, sticky little *petits fours* on silver platters that had only faint shadowings of tarnish mixed with polish in the embossments. All the foodstuffs my father most disliked, but it was the thought process that counted, and that had not been stinted. Aimée's hair sported a dash of pink too when you observed it closely: presumably the excitement of a male house-guest had sent her rushing to the henna pot.

Look who's talking: I had made a grudging effort myself, at least to the extent of changing out of my much criticised fisherman's jersey. I had always liked meeting my father when we had been separated for a while, always looked forward to it, even when I was officially at odds with him. Always looked forward to showing him off to people who didn't know him, catching their little starts of surprise and pleasure: he was so much taller than I, so much thinner and more elegant, it threw them. Those who did know him were fun to watch too – particularly the nuns when he used to come and fetch me from the convent. Nuns are not supposed to be flirty, but his presence set them fluttering like so many cooped-up chickens with a fox in the offing. The Reverend Mother, who in her Irishness shared his enthusiasm for the turf, once even greeted him by his nickname – although from her horror-struck expression afterwards I think it must have shot out by mistake. Not Michael, which would have been daring enough, but Mickey. This, just to show his appeal – how strong it was, and how it winged in on such varied targets, taking effect more or less right across the whole female board. Only my mother seemed to have eluded its range, but at prohibitive cost.

Aimée was *ravie* – that was her word for it, repeated endlessly over the next half-hour as, in the role of hostess, she greeted her guest, bustled him inside, plied him with food, showered him with compliments, showed him to his room and generally made an elaborate French fuss of him. Ravished, transported, enraptured, carried away. My own feeling of happiness was more down to earth: not a carrying away but a carrying towards. The moment I heard the wheels of the car on the gravel I rushed outside and, hardly waiting for my father to get out of the car, flew into his arms and buried my face in the folds of his beautiful cream silk shirt. A bit hot from the drive, but he smelt so nice, so familiar, so safe. These arms had shielded me before from a host of dangers – intrusive strangers, jealous dogs, stroppy yearlings, once even a furious plover whose nest I had trodden on by mistake – and just as surely they would shield me now.

When Aimée finally left us alone together I plumped myself down on the edge of the bed while he did his unpacking. It was amazing the amount of stuff he'd brought with him: even a dinner jacket, even his smart patent-leather evening shoes. And at his, Off you go then, my poor baba, tell me exactly what the trouble is, I went through the entire chronicle of my woes from start to finish.

He didn't comment except to frown a bit when I described Aimée's Peeping Puss habits during the *soirées*, didn't interrupt, didn't laugh, didn't do anything except go on quietly with his unpacking and let me talk.

When I'd finished, i.e. when the telling and reality intersected one another on the crux of the present moment – So *that's* what we're up against, you see. Three of them, if not four, if not more – he sat down beside me and took me into his arms and rocked me for a while, to and fro in very small excursions. An inch each way, if that.

My poor baba, my poor overwrought baba, what a lot goes through this busy old noddle.

A lot of nonsense is what you mean, I said, half-laughing, half-crying, still keeping my face turned inward, towards his chest.

His arms tightened around me. No, no, I never said that. I'm not going to *dis*believe you, my love. Never, never, never. I can see you're serious, can see you have worked yourself up into a big, big state about this poor sick friend of yours. On the other hand – and the hug grew just a fraction slacker so that I knew some kind of disavowal was coming – I'm not going to *be*lieve you either, not outright, not straight away, because you wouldn't really respect my judgement much if I did. Isn't that so? Well, isn't it? Be honest, isn't it?

I nodded, but more to please him than out of any conviction. What I would have preferred to see him do was what vampire-slayers did in films: whip out a hawthorn stake from his suitcase and brandish it in the air shouting, 'Tremble, vile creatures of the night!' But then, on reflection, perhaps not; perhaps a balanced approach was in the end more reassuring.

Good. That's more like my bottle. Now, listen, what I'm going to do is this: I'm going to *act* as if I believe you – all along the line. Right? Anything you want me to do – within reason. I'm not going round sticking wooden stakes into people at the drop of a hat, obviously not, but anything reasonable that you want me to do to make you feel protected against these fears of yours, real or imaginary, I will do. You want me to sit up all night outside the house of . . . what's her name again? . . . Sabine, and make sure no vampires climb up the drainpipe and no bats fly in her window? Fine, I will sit up. With my bat-swatter. You want me to try and persuade her mother to let her come and stay with us in England? No problem, I will do that too. You want me to stay on here with you till you feel safe about travelling? I brought the car for that very purpose. No ties, no tickets, we can leave when you are ready to do so and not before. Is that a bargain?

Yes, I said, and then corrected myself quickly. No, it wasn't, not yet, not until I heard my bargain part. He would do all this for me, and I loved him for it and was deeply, deeply grateful, but what did he want me to do in return?

Nothing, he said, just to be quiet and reasonable and stop letting my imagination run away with me. And not to do anything dotty in public to disgrace him, like panicking or screaming or throwing garlic round the shop or making wild accusations. He had been invited to the party at the de Vibreys' that evening, apparently. Now, the Marquis, vampire or not, was a friend, or at least a close acquaintance – he was in fact more of a friend of Teddy's but it came to much the same thing – and he was also stuffed to the gills with lovely foreign lolly, so the plan was to flog him a share in this colt he and

Teddy had recently bought together. Colts were so expensive to keep in training. Like boys. Much better to have bottles. *Provided* they kept their heads and didn't go to pieces at the sight of a dusty cat and some old newspaper cuttings. So, the bargain was this: I was to come along with him to the party on my best behaviour – yes, right into the vampire stronghold, if that was the way I wanted to put it. The son was bound to be there, so we needn't have any worries on that account, in fact it meant we could keep a closer eye on him – on the lot of them for that matter. And afterwards we would drive to Sabine's, if it would put my mind at rest, and spend the whole night there if necessary, sitting in the car, guarding the place against intruders.

I was almost reassured by this plan but not quite.

What if he comes, though? I said. What if Roland comes to Sabine's when we are there? What will you do to him? How will you stop him, when he's so much stronger? You haven't really been listening carefully to what I said about these creatures, have you? The rice, for example, the grainy material – we could take some of that to throw in his pathway if we get really stuck. Or else we could . . .

Viola, my love, I have lived a long, long time, much longer than you have. Do you trust your old dad, or don't you? Who took you to see those X-rated films when you were under age and gave you a cigarette to hold so that the girl at the box office would let you in? I did. Who watched while you hid your eyes in your hands, and told you what was going on? I did. Test me if you don't believe me. Tell me a procedure for tackling vampires that I don't know already. Go on, try me.

I was silent, running through the list of methods in my head. I could remember only four, all of them – except for the rice, which I had already mentioned – extremely well known, even to someone as vague on the subject as my father.

You see? You can't. I'll tell you one though which may make you laugh: they live so bloody long they can be killed by boredom.

XVIII

Homecoming

I f I think of that evening – force myself to think of
it, because no way can it float casually into my
mind like other thoughts: the barrier is far too thick
– I see the forecourt of the Château de Vibrey again,
emptier and darker than it was on the day of the
hunt, but still quite full, although of cars this time,
and still quite bright, even in its nocturnal dress. I
see the light of lantern flames licking against the
yews, turning the foliage a thick dark bronze that I
have only encountered before on ballet shoes, never
on leaves.

I see two liveried footmen on either side of the
curved stairway that leads to the entrance, looking
as if they have stepped from an illustrated fairy tale
and are dead ashamed of the fact, each holding
another lantern on a pole. I see light of a different
metallic hue, yellower, brassier, streaming from the
doors and windows and falling in colder, almost
moon-coloured, geometrical patterns on the flag-
stones. As we cross them I see the shine of my
father's patent-leather party slippers, hear them

emit a tiny squeak as he walks, and feel the dry warmth of his hand in mine. His hands are never sticky, not even on a torrid night like this one; his nails, though nicotiney, are always clean; he smells of scent and soap and tobacco smoke. The rich, solid, comforting, bourgeois smell of someone who knows how to tame a savage world and harness it to his advantage.

We are entering a dangerous place, an arena full of predators, maybe even a trap, but my trust in him is complete. As we mount the stairs, he and I in front, Christopher following with his parents (who look drab in comparison and out of place, having had no time to change), and Aimée in sequins twittering along behind, I think to myself that if he were to die, if my father were to die, I would feel as if there were no floor beneath my feet, no ground, no supporting surface at all; I would stagger and I would fall for ever. Quite apart from this rescue mission, which is hopefully a one-off, who would undo life's lesser knots for me when they snarled? Particularly the red-taped ones which scare me almost as badly. Who would check my bank statements? Who would know what debentures were? Who would speak to solicitors and lawyers? What if I get into debt and need to raise a mortgage? How on earth do you raise a mortgage and what do you do with it once it is risen? Last time I saw him, my heart full of Sabine, I thought I could do without him, but I see now I was wrong. The opposite is the case: without him I would lose everything, Sabine included.

I squeeze his hand and he squeezes mine back and whispers: What did the earwig say when he went over the cliff? (He loves daft jokes like that. A mean old Count. My enema the douche. Nicholas II was bizarre.)

Earwigo, I reply, all dutiful and conniving again, as if I had never been otherwise.

Earwigo, then.

And we step through the portals of the Vampires' Castle, under the noses of a second pair of unhappy torch-bearers – no, halberd-bearers in this instance – and into the fray.

Polanski's film with the famous ball scene came out years later, so I can't have been reminded of it then, but my mind now serves me up a false and vivid impression that I was. There were no mirrors to betray us, all wall-space being given over to those ubiquitous gory Gobelin hangings of the chase – a *galerie de chasses* and not *de glaces* – and yet I remember clearly, or think I do, that my first act on entering was to look round for one in terror, convinced that, as it was for Polanski's hapless vampire-hunters, it would be the medium of our downfall. Why this pastiche? Why this confusion? Simple, because in common with the film's characters – no matter how much later on I saw it – I had that same feeling of nakedness, of exposure, of being part of a tiny camouflaged minority whose cover may at any moment be blown. 'All eyes turned to look at us' would be a slipshod way of putting it; eyes don't turn anyway, heads do, but as our little group joined the fringe of the assembly, there was a discernible swivelling of attention in our direction. I caught several haughty looks, disparaging but curious all the same. What-has-the-cat-brought-in looks, I am tempted to call them, seeing that it was Aimée who effectively ushered us into the room, only now there is no more time for word games, we are drawing too close to the quick.

Rapid assessment of numbers was not as then my forte. It was not a big gathering though, that much I could tell – thirty-five, forty people, fifty at the outside. Their ages? Well, of course that's a difficult one to establish, always, but I would say, trying to look back without the interference of hindsight, that what struck me even then was the middling nature of the age factor: no old people and, apart from Christopher and myself and the de Vibrey offspring, very few young either.

Middling, too, was almost every other aspect of their appearance. I'd been keyed up for the Grand Vampire Jamboree, and was still hanging on to my father's hand on that account, much as if, like Theseus with his ball of string, my safe delivery from danger depended on this link alone, but after a few seconds' observation I found myself shaking free quite spontaneously in order not to look foolish in his eyes. Or anyone else's for that matter. What had I expected? Exactly what my film-fed imagination had led me to expect: i.e. first and foremost glamour, style, no matter how crummy such details as hemlines and fingernails might turn out to be on close inspection. I had pictured to myself reds, purples, silks, velvets, boas, shawls, the works. Colours in superabundance: long amber cigarette holders resting on vermilion lips, wings of peacock-blue eyeshadow over black-rimmed bloodshot eyes. That was the hallmark of the vampire community, surely? Their dash, their campness, their love of the baroque.

Here, instead, was provincial *comme il faut* France. A parcel of trim cocktail-dressed women, sleek and black and uniform as starlings, interspersed with, rather on the poultry side, a sprinkling of dowdy Mme de Vallemberts in beige brocade plus pearls. The male contingent even drabber. Dr la Forge and two dozen or so replicas of same – professionals, notaries, notables – hardly noticeable at all in their dark crocheted ties and grey pinstripe suits. Monochrome were it not for, on this or that sober lapel, the minute red button of the *Légion d'Honneur* bleeping its discreet signal of distinction. True, Aimée's sequins added a bit of glitter, and the Marquis was wearing a velvet smoking jacket, but it was matt and mole-coloured and gave off not a spark of panache until you got close enough to see the material. And even that looked too new for real elegance.

The Marquis clasped my father in a politician's bear hug, empty and showy (or so it seemed to me), making urgent signals with his eyebrows to the Marquise over my father's shoulder. *Le cher Miqui, le cher Miqui. Enfin, ici, chez nous.* I could well imagine both husband and wife referring to him in private as a parvenu. When, after greeting Christopher's parents and granting another half-hug to Aimée, who nearly climaxed in consequence, he turned his attention to me, I bowed my head in apparent modesty, but in fact in order to avoid another nose-tap. Anything but that, you old smoothie, I thought, even my jugular but not that.

We are so delighted to have you all with us on this . . . this . . . ah, well, I'll save my oratory till we come to the toasts – this very *special* evening. Is that not so, my dear?

The Marquise, who had joined us with a rapid glide after the semaphore business with the eyebrows, nodded and bared a set of regular and pretty teeth that didn't deceive me for an instant. To be that rude and that polite together must take, literally, centuries of practice. She extended fingertips all round, blowing a tiny long-distance kiss to my father when she came to him; it was a wonder it didn't freeze his cheek.

So glad you could make the voyage. You poor English with your currency regulations – it would depress me *de manière folle*. No shopping in Paris, no skiing in the winter – how do you manage, how do you manage?

We manage thanks to kind, hospitable friends like yourselves. My father slid these words in quickly, suppository fashion: too early yet to bring up the racehorse deal but no harm preparing the way. I had been embarrassed at the thought of hearing him struggle along in French, but really he spoke the language passably well. Which came as a relief because embarrassment would have weakened our position; with these creatures, whether vampires or just snooty fuddy-duddies looking down their Gallic noses at us, we needed to dominate for comfort.

Ah, Miqui, toujours le galant.

Etcetera, etceterbla. The evening got under way and proceeded on its stuffy and quite uneventful course. Eats of a dainty but slightly papier-mâché variety were carried around by white-gloved waiters. Among them I recognised some of the hunt-servants: they had fed the hounds, maybe the horses too, and now they were feeding us. Be thankful therefore for the gloves. My legs started tingling from standing on one spot, and my jaw began to have that achy feeling brought about by too much inane smiling. Talking might have helped to relax the muscles, but there was nobody friendly to talk to – except Christopher, and he was still giving me the pariah treatment. I had entered the room half paralysed by fear; I risked leaving it almost totally paralysed by boredom. (Leaving it, but when? When? Where *had* my father got to? Ah, there he was, talking to Christopher's mum. He looked as despairing as I felt, why wasn't he picking up my distress signals so we could bolt?)

Roland was present, as we had anticipated, wedged in a far corner with a couple of aldermen or suchlike, looking dutiful to the point of preppy, so I didn't even have the worry of his whereabouts to keep me on edge. He'd given me another of those strange looks of his when he saw me – sweet, wistful, almost pitying – it made me think with a twinge of discomfort that I still hadn't really figured him out at all. We were rivals. Rivals for Sabine, and I stood slap in his path. Last night I had thwarted him, outwitted him, and tonight with my reinforcements I would do worse: he ought to resent me, surely? But no, there he was, all smiles and solidarity. Devious beast. Slippery, reptilian hybrid or whatever you could call him. My father would settle him, though. It was enough to look from one to the other and compare their stances – Roland's, poised, light, hesitant, rocking slightly from heel to toe; my father's, confidently planted on the ground – to realise that, wherever a future conflict between the two might take place, there was no question who would emerge from it victorious. Creature of the night versus man of the world. No contest even: the man of the world would win, hands down, feet down.

Rap, rap, rap. Interruption – so welcome that it felt like rescue at the time – came at length from one of the halberdiers, who had mounted a kind of dais at the back of the gallery and was now banging the staff of his halberd on the floorboards, requesting silence in a booming voice.

Silence took some time coming. Nobody appeared willing to heed the command of a social inferior. After the surprise of the first spate of bangs everyone just shrugged and went on talking – that much louder to cover the din – and it was not until the Marquis himself stepped on to the dais and instigated a pleading action with a decidedly personal touch that gradually, starting with those nearest to him and then fanning out ripple-wise to the rest, quiet was established and his voice became audible.

My friends, he began, those few of you who can read my handwriting will already know why we are gathered here this evening, heh, heh, but it is my pleasure nonetheless to announce to you the reason with the due touch of ceremony that such news deserves. The more so because in the meantime another piece of good news, of a more private nature, has added itself to the first, giving us double cause for celebration. I will begin with this second announcement. Unfortunately, owing to the dictates of convalescence – by which I mean the dictates of our dear Doctor here, so punctilious, so *rigoureux* . . . (there followed a moment's pause as the Marquis sought out and indicated a perspiring la Forge among the listeners, and waited for laughter that was not forthcoming). *Un*fortunately, he resumed, neither the charming young lady concerned, nor her equally enchanting mother, could be here tonight in person to share our joy, but they are here with us in spirit. My son Roland will be joining them shortly and will convey to them the *félicitations*, I am sure, of us all. Together with . . . (At this he held up his left hand and made a stroking gesture of his ring finger with the right, bringing from his audience, all except me, a chorus of dutiful Ahs.) Because, yes, indeed, my friends, you have guessed correctly, this is the announcement I have to make on behalf of myself and my wife and which makes us both so happy and proud: the betrothal of our son Roland to Mademoiselle Marie Sabine de la Cour d'Houanche.

I felt as if someone had ripped out my innards. Empty inside, and yet full of pain to come. The man was lying, he must be. They were cheating, all of them, they must be. Sabine would never have consented to an engagement – with no matter whom – without discussing her intention with me first. Or telling me about it, at the very least. In her right mind she would never have consented to an engagement, full stop. It was all a lie, a put-up job, there was not a word of truth in anything the Marquis said.

Then I remembered Ghislaine's smile that morning when speaking of the *réception*, and the announced pain flooded in with a whoosh, almost winding me with its violence. It was true without a doubt. Ghislaine knew and she was thrilled to bits about it, and she hadn't dared tell me and no wonder. When could it have happened? When could this terrible thing have happened? Not today for sure – Roland hadn't been to see Sabine yet. Yesterday then. Yesterday when she was a helpless doll. The doll had got engaged, not Sabine. The doll had been pressed into an engagement.

Around me everyone was clapping and making buzzing noises of congratulation. The footmen/ huntsmen were whirling in, trays of champagne glasses held high above their heads. On his platform the Marquis was waving his hands around again, trying to indicate that he hadn't yet finished what he had to say, but with scant success. The buzz grew and the glasses were grabbed and filled and raised and emptied and refilled. I stood there in misery, explanations and excuses flashing across my mind and then fizzling out like spent fireworks: I rejected all of them. Didn't even deign to follow their course. Oh, I knew with my reason that Sabine was beyond blame, but who can reason on the rack? Whatever comforting slant I might attempt to put on it, the bare, unalterable fact remained: she had ultimately chosen him, Roland, in preference to me, and – far graver treachery in my view – had not so much as bothered to inform me of her choice. Indeed, she had done worse: that morning when I had kissed her, she had actually turned away in order to prevent me from reading the truth on her face, knowing as well as I did that her eyes could never lie, closed lids and all. Hence Roland's pity – he could afford it.

I was so numbed, so stunned, the hurt of Sabine's silence had cut so deep, that even when the room fell quiet enough again for the Marquis to be heard, the remainder of his words were lost to me. I could see, and I could hear, and to outward appearances I could still function, but inside me some vital mechanism of comprehension seemed to have jammed. It was like watching a movie in an unknown foreign language. (And who knows, maybe it was better that way too. A jab of anaesthetic given me by a merciful Nurse Chance.)

My main preoccupation anyway was keeping check on Roland's movements – nothing else really mattered. Shortly, we had been informed, he would be setting out to join Sabine. How short was shortly? How much time did my father and I have in which to foil him? We must get to Sabine's home before he did; it was no good arriving later, even five minutes' delay might be fatal, even four, even one: she was so weak now she would hardly survive another bleeding. At present he was easy enough to monitor because the whole de Vibrey brood, daughters included, had now mounted the dais and were standing there on either side of their parents, champagne glasses at the ready, clinking and drinking in unison like a row of mass-manoeuvred puppets. The toasts, that was it, this must be the moment of the toasts. But once he left the platform it would be hard to keep track of him in the confusion. He could easily slip away without my noticing, and then . . .

Oh, the follow-on was intolerable, unthinkable. The ring, the pledge, the promise . . . His strength, his swoop; her weakness, her surrender . . . Oh no. Oh no, it must be stopped, it must be stopped. I cast around urgently for my father only to realise, with a gush of relief, that he was standing right behind me and had in fact placed a protective hand on my shoulder which I, in my stupefied state, had failed to notice. I tugged at one of the fingers to attract his attention but he drummed it against mine reprovingly and made a hissing noise: he was listening to the Marquis's speech with what was, for him, a fairly good forgery of rapt attention. I looked round and up at him a second time, examining him closer: his face was creased in a polite society smile, eyes faintly glazed over with tedium and the desire to hide it. His other hand, with a wine glass in it, went up and down in synchrony with all the others. Why, I wondered, when by inclination he was so detached and ironic, was he at bottom such a conformist? His heroes were Byron and Disraeli: perhaps that afforded a key. They too had been romantic about things like wealth and lineage, they too had been torn between contempt of public opinion and servitude to its laws. The genial cripple and the genial Jew: two stars so uncertain of their shine that they needed a reflecting surface, even though it was only the lid of an old tin can and they knew it. Was my father perhaps the same? Uncertain? Insecure despite all his apparent assurance?

Oh, I hate the way these smug old maxims always turn out to be true: *Tout comprendre c'est tout pardonner*. Does this mean I must forgive him everything? No, it means I must take a step further and recognise there's nothing *to* forgive: things go as they will go.

The Marquis had finished proposing toasts now and was making a different set of gestures. Beckoning gestures, master-of-ceremony gestures, come-on-everybody-let's-get-going gestures. Rather vulgar for an aristocrat, but then he was a vulgar man, title and all. At the rear of the dais one of the footmen was trafficking with a gramophone and a pile of records. I saw the Marquis point to him and then turn to his audience and shrug, hands spread in apology, as much as to say, Once upon a time we would have had a proper orchestra, even for a cocktail party, now all I can offer is this.

He mouthed a few short words, looking straight at my father, and from above my head my father nodded approval and mouthed them back. I know now what they were, which means I must have lip-read them and filed them away in my mind for later interpretation. They were in English: 'Smoke Gets in Your Eyes'.

At the time, though, I don't think I heard either them or the music they were set to, nor felt my father's arms around me as he swung me to face him and swept me on to the dance floor in full view of all the onlookers. I'm not sure I even felt the puncture of his teeth as they sank deep into my neck, or heard the gentle apology-cum-warning that may or may not have preceded it, or the applause that followed – generally pretty raucous on such occasions, going by later experience. I'm not sure, I'm not sure. It sounds improbable, but my attention was still focused on Roland, on making sure I kept him in my sights.

I remember putting my hand to my neck distractedly, and bringing it away smeared with blood, and looking at it for an instant in puzzlement, and then up at my father, and noticing that he too had blood on his face, and thinking nothing, nothing at all except, Well, so what; we can wash when we get to Sabine's. I remember, too, out of the corner of my eye, seeing Christopher in much the same messy state shuffling around awkwardly with his mum in a kind of fractious foxtrot, and being grateful that at least we had company and were not the only couple to be cutting such a dismal figure in front of our *grenouille* hosts. Although, mind you, the Marquis, as he slid by with his youngest daughter in tow, didn't look exactly all that pristine around the jaws himself.

Roland was dancing, not with his mother, as

might have been expected for reasons of symmetry if nothing else, but with one of his elder sisters. My concentration still fixed on him almost exclusively, I saw him yawn and consult his watch behind his sister's back. Then he whispered something to her, and the two of them loosened hands and drew apart, and I saw him dig into one of his pockets and extract from it a bunch of keys. The keys to the car. He was going. There was no time to lose: we must act immediately.

He's leaving! I said to my father, shaking his hand in order to rouse him, and then, when this didn't work, digging at his shins with my knee. Roland's *leaving*! He's making for Sabine's. We've got to go. We've got to get there first, remember? Remember? You promised, remember?

My father's face, in addition to the bloodstain, wore a faraway, bleary look when finally he glanced down at me. He seemed to be awaking from a reverie or sobering up after a soak. Instead of interrupting the dance he clasped me tighter and bent his head so that it was practically touching my ear. To his credit, I think I heard a break in his voice when he spoke.

Let him go, my darling, he said. Let him go to this Sabine you love so much, and let him do what he wants to her. Better him than you. Believe me, better him than you.

Yes, crazy though it sounds, it was not until my father spoke – these words that I actually could hear, as opposed to mere mouthings – that, slowly, slowly, as I shuffled around the floor to the dance music, trapped in his arms like the prisoner I now was, the truth came home to me.

Coda

I use the term 'came home' with irony but also with resignation. Because that is what that evening was about, you see, that is what we were celebrating: a coming-out in society that was at the same time a homecoming, a welcome to the fold.

Meaning that your rival won her in the end? (It is the voice of the man in the picture again, his image surfacing in my mind again after another interval of decades.) That beautiful girl you were both so fond of – you lost her, and he won?

I hesitate a moment before replying because this time he is only partly right. I lost Sabine, but Roland didn't win her, not really, not for long. She died in May of the following year – of a haemorrhage resulting from a miscarriage, or so the official story went. I have difficulty believing it, but even if true, it makes no difference to the way I view her executioner: greedy parasite or ardent husband, he still bled her to death. I also heard talk that her end was unintentional – a foul-up by the leaders of the vampire community, who didn't bother to brief

Roland properly on his task before letting him loose on her: No bingeing, young man, just keep her out of the way till we've got things settled with the other girl – our new recruit. *Surtout pas trop de zèle.* But that doesn't make any difference to the way I view things either: they wanted to split us, Sabine and me, and split us they did.

The man of the portrait listens sympathetically, smiling his gently ironic smile. And what about you, Viola? he asks, when I've finished. What happened to you?

I went on to become a doctor, I tell him, though my reasons for this choice of career were vague. It could have been because the profession, with its handy blood supply, provides a simple way of procuring nourishment for those of my kind, or it could have been that I felt (mistakenly, as it turned out) that it would continue to connect me somehow to Sabine. Oh, that Italian song, how sad its words are. The world that is; the world that could have been. My life as I live it now; my life as we could have lived it, Sabine and I together. When I think of my loss . . .

Your loss? The man of the portrait interrupts me, lifting a painted eyebrow that turns his ironic gaze to one of overt cynicism. Oh, come now, Viola, your relationship was far too conflictual, it never would have worked. Two young women bickering over the young men who come between them; two middle-aged women bickering over futilities; then two old women bickering over the shreds of their empty existence – that is the way it would have been. You have conserved your dream intact. Be content with that.

Is a dream more precious, then, than reality? I ask.

The canvas smile only intensifies, as much as to say: You are the dream expert, Viola, you know the answer.

A Note on the Type

The text of this book is set in Linotype Sabon,
named after the type founder, Jacques Sabon. It
was designed by Jan Tschichold and jointly
developed by Linotype, Monotype and Stempel,
in response to a need for a typeface to be available
in identical form for mechanical hot-metal
composition and hand composition using
foundry type.

Tschichold based his design for Sabon roman on
a fount engraved by Garamond, and Sabon italic
on a fount by Granjon. It was first used in 1966
and has proved an enduring modern classic.